“Logan Wi
A Cheap Womanizer?

“Not cheap,” came a vibrant, laughing voice from behind her. “I may be guilty of a wealth of vices, Miss Yorke—but being cheap is not among them.”

“Logan Wilde,” she whispered despairingly.

“Guilty as charged. And you’re Cassidy Yorke—even more attractive in the flesh, I may add, than on the screen.”

He was taller than she’d imagined, and broader through the shoulders, leaner through the hips. The smile was the same though . . . easy and warm, and infinitely inviting.

“Do I pass muster, Miss Yorke?” he asked with a husky laugh. “If you see something you particularly like, just say the word and I’ll be glad to arrange for a closer inspection. Because,” he added in that silken purr, “you certainly pass mine.”

Dear Reader:

SILHOUETTE DESIRE is an exciting new line of contemporary romances from Silhouette Books. During the past year, many Silhouette readers have written in telling us what other types of stories they'd like to read from Silhouette, and we've kept these comments and suggestions in mind in developing SILHOUETTE DESIRE.

DESIREs feature all of the elements you like to see in a romance, plus a more sensual, provocative story. So if you want to experience all the excitement, passion and joy of falling in love, then SILHOUETTE DESIRE is for you.

For more details write to:

Jane Nicholls
Silhouette Books
PO Box 236
Thornton Road
Croydon
Surrey CR9 3RU

NAOMI HORTON

Split Images

Silhouette Desire

Originally Published by Silhouette Books
division of
Harlequin Enterprises Ltd.

I came to KALB—and a week hasn't gone by since that I haven't been out there covering one world-shaking event or another. Half those animals out there think I'm one of the keepers!" Marsh grinned and Cassidy laughed, shaking her head. "Sorry. I shouldn't be taking this out on you—but I get so frustrated! Every time I try to do a story that's even remotely serious, the fifth floor shoots me down. Or they let me do it, and it never airs."

"Patience, darling," he murmured consolingly. "It all takes time, you know. After all, *Cassidy's Corner* is still in the experimental stage. Your main job's still news reporting. You have two prime-time spots, which is nothing to scoff at."

Cassidy shot him an impatient look. "*News* reporting, Marsh? I read a prepared transcript twice a day. Any idiot can sit in front of a camera and read a piece of paper."

Marsh raised an expressive eyebrow. "I still say it's not too bad for someone who only ten months ago was reporting the weather in a no-name station in the backwoods of Oregon."

Cassidy opened her mouth for an impatient reply, then closed it again with a sigh. It wasn't Marsh's fault. He simply didn't understand that it just wasn't enough. She was busy, yes, but it was all lightweight material, most of it prepared by someone else and simply handed to her before she went on the air. She did all her own research and legwork for *Cassidy's Corner*, of course, but even that didn't give her the solid, hard reporting she wanted. The couple of times she had tried to cover anything of real importance, she'd either been told to drop it, or her videotape had simply vanished into the depths of the library, never to be seen.

"Well, darling," Marsh concluded, slipping off the desk, "I must run. I want to review my notes before I go on. You *are* going to watch my interview tonight, aren't you? It's going to be a dilly!"

Cassidy swallowed a sigh. "You're interviewing the president of Eclipse Corporation, aren't you? About that land development deal that's causing all the ruckus at City Hall?"

"That's the one. I've uncovered a sweetheart deal between Eclipse and a couple of honorable members of City Council. It would appear—" he leaned forward slightly, his voice taking on a conspiratorial tone "—that one or two of said honorable members made a killing when that land was sold. *Someone* had inside information." He gave a knowing nod, then, catching sight of someone over Cassidy's head, he straightened. "Well, darling, have a good show. Jeri? Jeri, don't you ignore me!" He hurried off, Cassidy already forgotten. "Jeri, we really must talk about the color of the backdrop on the new set!"

Cassidy shook her head ruefully, unable to subdue entirely the tiny stab of envy that shot through her at the thought of Marsh's interview. Getting the president of Eclipse Corporation to sit still for a television interview was a major coup. Every news team in every station in New Mexico had been trying for months, ever since the first whiff of scandal had broken. All had failed. For Marsh to have succeeded was as much a feather in KALB's cap as it was in his own. They were still the new kid on the block, the newest station to enter the cutthroat market for Albuquerque viewers. But they were coming up fast. Shows like *Headliners* were making sure of that.

"Ready for your first big celebrity interview, Cass?"

Cassidy looked around to see the show's executive producer, Ken Vaughn, approaching. He was the picture of the successful young executive on his way up. Slim, fit and well tanned, he looked as though he'd just come from a meeting with all big three networks on New York's Sixth Avenue. It was a goal, Cassidy knew, that was never far from his thoughts.

"I may have a no-show," she replied hopefully.

Ken's lean face broke into a smile. "Someone called to say Wilde's plane just landed. I sent a car out to pick him up, but—" he looked at his watch "—it's going to be tight."

"It would be a real shame if he didn't make it, wouldn't it?" Cassidy offered pleasantly.

Ken sighed. "Let's not go through this again. You said you wanted something different. I gave you something different."

"Interviewing the world's quintessential playboy bachelor is not quite what I had in mind," she advised him pointedly. "And I don't understand why I'm doing it anyway. This type of celebrity interview is right up Marsh Wheeler's alley. When Wilde's name first came up at that planning meeting a month ago, as a matter of fact, it was Marsh's story."

Ken paused very slightly. "Marsh has been tied up on this Eclipse story. And the boys upstairs figured it would be more effective to have a woman interview Wilde." He smiled. "Wilde's appeared on every major talk show in the country since his new book hit the stands. It's about time he showed up on the screen in his home town. You should be flattered he agreed to do the show, honey. The competition's been fighting tooth and nail to sign him up." He caught her look and held up both hands, grinning apologetically. "Sorry! I know I promised not to call you 'honey' anymore. It just slipped out."

In spite of herself, Cassidy found herself laughing. Ken was impossible. "Well, it's academic if he doesn't get here in time. I'll do the *Headliners* intro with Marsh as usual. If Wilde hasn't turned up by then, I'll do a quick on-air explanation. Then why don't we run that special I did last month on the water crisis in Taos, the one Crothers axed for being 'too controversial'? If we slip it in fast enough, it'll be on-air before he realizes what's happening." She grinned recklessly. "Then I'll make myself very scarce until the post-show wrap-up."

Ken looked at her for a moment. "I don't think so," he said quietly. "If Wilde doesn't show, we're going to run that tape on your zoo tour. It's always popular."

Cassidy stared at him. "Darn it, Ken, that Taos special is important! Even Dick agreed that—"

"Dick Craig's just the director," Ken reminded her with the faintest hint of coolness. "He controls the cameras; I control the show."

And the fifth floor controls you, she very nearly added. She swallowed the barb, knowing that Ken Vaughn hated the restrictions put on them by the programming executives and owners as much as she did.

"Cheer up, Cass," he teased. "I'll get that special on for you one of these days. Trust me."

"Don't patronize me, Ken," Cassidy said with quiet precision. "You know as well as I do that the special will never be aired. Why don't you just come out and admit it instead of playing games with me?"

Ken managed to look sincerely hurt. "You don't know that for certain, Cass!"

"Oh, come off it, Ken!" she snapped, patience gone. "You've been promising me for weeks that you'd talk to Crothers about changing the format of *Headliners* to give me more serious work. And I haven't seen anything yet to indicate you've done it. Why should I start believing you now?"

"Cass!" He held out his hands placatingly. "Honey, we've been all through this before. If it was just between you and me, I'd change the show's format in a minute. But the boys on the fifth floor call the shots. You know that. They feel we're giving the audience exactly what it wants now, and they don't want to play around with success."

"Ken, *Headliners* could be one of the top news shows in the country if we got rid of all the cutesy fluff and concentrated on issues that matter!"

He held up both hands again, this time in surrender. "Cass, I know how you feel. But people don't want hard issues when they're eating dinner. We're offering them something light, something fun." He grinned engagingly. "Besides, people don't tune in *Headliners* for the news, they tune in to see you—the most gorgeous face on television. You make them laugh, Cassidy. You make them feel good. Now tell me, what's wrong with that?"

"If I was interested in making people laugh," she stated with forced calm, "I'd have become a stand-up comedian. I've had about all I can take of performing cats, would-be magicians and every eccentric who crawls out of the woodwork claiming to be Howard Hughes's long lost son, or the rightful heir to the throne of England!"

"Cass, you've got to be patient. Crothers feels you need more seasoning, that's all. More on-air time. Besides, I don't know why you can't be satisfied with being the most popular lady in town. Your show's a hit!"

Cassidy looked at him impatiently. "What Crothers really means is that television is still a man's game. I sometimes think that the only reason he hired me was because I'm female and he'd been getting flack from the union about having no woman on-air."

"Now, Cassidy," Ken protested with a mollifying smile. "Jack Crothers might not be the most enlightened man in New Mexico, but he wouldn't have hired you if he didn't think you were damn good at what you do."

"Then why doesn't he—" Cassidy caught herself, realizing it was a futile battle. She thought of the letter in her briefcase, the one that had come from the big Seattle station that wanted to hire her. She'd planned on showing it to Ken today, hoping it might jolt him into realizing how serious she was about easing *Cassidy's Corner* away from the frothy silliness they'd been doing lately and into something that mattered. Then she sighed wearily. It wasn't quite time to play her hand yet, she decided, not until she'd given the whole thing more thought. "I'll play along with it for a while longer, Ken. But don't count on that keeping me in line indefinitely. Because contract or no contract, I'm not going to let KALB hold back my career if I get the opportunity to do something better."

Ken looked at her sharply, eyes narrowing. “Are you telling me someone’s trying to hire you away from KALB?”

“I’m just telling you that people are starting to take notice, Ken,” she told him calmly. “I do good work, you know that. Maybe it’s time the fifth floor took notice, too.” Then she sat up, setting her notes aside and looking up at the big clock. “I’m on in eight minutes, and I’ve got to brush my hair and put on fresh lipstick.” She smiled sweetly. “After all, we must give the audience what it wants, mustn’t we?” She laughed quietly at the expression on Ken’s face. “Oh, don’t worry, Ken, I’m not going on-air to accuse KALB of sexual discrimination. But you might want to remind Jack Crothers that I did not join this station to be just another pretty talking head. *Headliners* is supposed to be a news support show, not another prime-time entertainment program.”

“Logan Wilde *is* news,” he reminded her gently.

“Logan Wilde,” Cassidy stated emphatically, “is a chauvinist and a cheap womanizer. He has the ethics, morals and sensitivity of a weasel and is about as relevant to modern day relationships as chastity belts and harems!”

“Not cheap,” came a vibrant, laughing voice from behind her. “I may be guilty of a wealth of vices, Miss Yorke, but being cheap is not among them.”

Cassidy swallowed a gasp and whirled around to find herself being lazily inspected by two of the bluest eyes she’d ever encountered in her life. A man was standing there, tall and lean and relaxed, smiling down at her. He was casually dressed, but deceptively so: the jeans were designer label, the cream and blue pullover and coordinated blue shirt subtly expensive, the suede desert boots handmade. He was holding a soft leather jacket the color of tobacco over his right shoulder, and she could see a flash of Cartier gold at his wrist where his cuff had pulled back.

“Logan Wilde,” she whispered despairingly. There was no doubt about it: clean-cut features straight and even, curling black hair meticulously styled, strong mouth tilted to one side in a come-hither smile that hit a perfect balance between blatant sensuousness and boyish charm.

"Guilty as charged." His smile widened and he extended his hand. "And you're Cassidy Yorke, even more attractive in the flesh, I may add, than on the screen." His voice was a liquid purr of sound, sensuously husky. His fingers folded warmly and firmly around hers, his grasp more a lover's caress than a handshake.

He was taller than she'd imagined. And broader through the shoulders, leaner through the hips. In fact, he looked like he would be more comfortable on the back of a horse than in the fast foreign cars he apparently favored. The smile was the same, though, she decided. Easy and warm and infinitely inviting . . .

"Do I pass muster, Miss Yorke?" he asked with a throaty laugh. "If you see something you particularly like, just say the word and I'll be glad to arrange a closer inspection." His blue eyes held hers boldly. "Because," he added in that silken purr, "you certainly pass mine."

Cassidy was astonished to feel her cheeks color. She'd expected Wilde to play his sexual games with her, but she hadn't expected the first move quite this soon. But of course he would, she realized. He would want to set the ground rules, the battle lines, within the first minutes of their meeting. It was about power, not sex. About control. Control of the situation, of the interview, of her. She'd seen the results on the many videotapes she'd watched—how he manipulated the tone and content of the interview, how he exerted subtle control over the questions and the questioner. But even though she was prepared for it, she found herself off balance. He was standing too close, deliberately crowding her, his thumb caressing the back of her hand lightly.

Cassidy held her ground, fighting the instinctive desire to step back. She withdrew her hand, staring up into those blue, blue eyes without a tremor. "You haven't given us much time to preview the show, Mr. Wilde," she said, deciding her best weapon was cool professionalism. "I hope you're familiar with our format."

"Unscheduled delay in L.A.," he explained lazily. "And I know your format inside out, Miss Yorke. I never miss a show. It's one of the best on the air."

Cassidy felt a little stab of pleasure until she realized that he was simply playing his games with her. Book Two, Chapter One, she reminded herself dryly: *any woman responds well to flattery*. "Try again," she murmured half to herself, trying not to smile.

"Sorry?"

Cassidy succumbed fully to the smile, looking straight into those improbably-blue eyes. "Nothing, Mr. Wilde. Just a note to myself." Still smiling, she sat back on the edge of her desk, arms folded. "I'm glad you could make it. I'd just about decided I'd have to do the show alone tonight."

"Not a chance," he murmured huskily. "I've been looking forward to this for weeks." Somehow, he managed to imbue the words with such undisguised sexuality that Cassidy blushed uncontrollably again.

"Four minutes, Miss Yorke!"

The loud voice startled Cassidy. She pushed herself away from the desk, knowing that Wilde was watching her like a cat with a mouse. One corner of that firm mouth tipped slowly upward in a self-satisfied smile as he realized he'd finally managed to get a reaction from her. Furious with Wilde, and with herself for being so ridiculously vulnerable, she took a deep breath, fighting an uncharacteristic urge to plant her open palm smartly across that handsome, mocking face. She gave Mike Szaski, the assistant director, a wave of acknowledgment. "That means you have about eight minutes before you're on, Mr. Wilde," she said crisply, already sensing that this interview was going to be every bit as distasteful as she'd anticipated. "I think you already know Ken Vaughn, our executive producer. I'll leave you in his capable hands while I get over to the set before the director and crew have a fit."

"Given a choice," Wilde purred, "I'd rather spend the evening in your capable hands." His amused eyes met hers with bold familiarity. "By the way, what do I call you? Cass? Cassie?"

Somehow, Cassidy managed to hold that challenging stare, realizing that if she showed the slightest sign of intimidation now the entire interview was doomed. This was her show, her interview, and Logan Wilde had better get that through his arrogant head right at the start. And there was no better time to teach him who was in charge, she decided grimly, than right now. "My name," she said with quiet precision, "is Cassidy. But you, Mr. Wilde, may call me Miss Yorke." Then, ignoring Ken's querulous mutter of protest, she turned and strode across to the *Headliners* set.

Sprawled comfortably in his tweed armchair, Marsh looked up at her. "You look mad enough to char wood. You and Vaughn been going at it again?"

"The man's impossible!" Cassidy replied furiously.

"Vaughn?"

"Logan Wilde!" Cassidy secured the tiny microphone to the neckline of her pale peach silk blouse, wishing she'd had time to freshen her lipstick. One of the stagehands appeared magically beside her with a hairbrush, and she snatched it gratefully and gave her shoulder length mane of curly chestnut hair a couple of hurried strokes. She handed it back to the young woman with a smile of thanks just as the floor director held up both hands, fingers spread, to indicate they had ten seconds to airtime.

The darkness behind the wall of glaring lights and equipment was alive with scurrying shadows. Camera operators, lighting technicians and other crew members moved with silent and swift competence, looking alien under the telephone headsets that linked them with the glassed-in control room overlooking the set. "Okay, guys," someone shouted. "Clear the set!"

Marsh sat up, adjusting his already perfect tie. "Remember this is supposed to be a friendly interview," he murmured, already smiling into the camera. "You look ready to draw blood."

Five seconds. Four. "Don't worry, Marsh," Cassidy breathed, her own mouth turning up in a welcoming smile. "I'm not going to steal your thunder. I'll be as inoffensive as always." A shadow moved in the dimness behind the lights just to her left. It was one shadow among many, yet something made her glance toward it. Instinct, perhaps, some prickling awareness of being watched, of being stalked. Her heart gave a thump as her gaze met Logan Wilde's unexpectedly. He smiled a private, slow smile that was for her alone. *Challenge accepted*, it seemed to say. *And the next move is mine*.

Then the red light on Camera One flicked on. "Good evening," she said warmly into the waiting lens. "My name's Cassidy Yorke, and this is *Headliners*."

The two-minute introduction went smoothly, with Marsh's requisite compliment on how attractive she was, the casual banter and chitchat, then her smiling reminder that *Cassidy's Corner* would be right back as they broke for station identification and commercials.

The red light went off. Marsh's smile vanished with it. "Damn it, Cass," he complained as he got to his feet, "you left the script twice! And that last crack about my tie—"

"Sorry," Cassidy murmured, feeling a flicker of irritation at the unmistakable whine in Marsh's voice. He would be complaining to Ken as usual. Ken would come to her after the show, smiling apologetically as he told her that Marsh had yet another burr under his blanket and could she *please* not go out of her way to annoy him for the next couple of days? She smiled. Poor Ken. Marsh was the closest thing to a big-name star that KALB had, and it fell to Ken to keep him happy.

There was a flurry of activity around her. One stagehand whisked Marsh's chair off the set as another moved in with the yucca palm that was supposed to give her show a homey touch. Three copies of Wilde's books appeared on the coffee table, artfully arranged to show their titles. Wilde himself materialized without warning, seating himself comfortably on the long sofa beside her. Frowning, he fumbled with the microphone as he tried to secure it to his shirt.

He finally held it out to Cassidy in defeat. "Give me a hand with this. It needs a woman's touch."

Cassidy had her mouth open to suggest he get one of the sound techs to help him when the twenty-second call came. "Give it to me!" She slid nearer to him and snatched it from his hand. Trying to ignore the distracting proximity of that smiling, handsome face, she slipped two well manicured fingers between the first and second buttons on his shirtfront. Her nails scraped through a tangle of coarse chest hair and Wilde winced.

"Hey!" he protested in a laughing growl, catching her hand in his. "Gently, darling, gently."

Startled, Cassidy looked up. His breath was warm and sweet on her mouth, and his eyes! They weren't simply blue, she decided dazedly, they were the color of crushed violets, the color of deep Caribbean seas at midnight. They were eyes that could see through to the soul's core, eyes that a woman could lose herself in.

His mouth curved in a smile mere inches from hers. "I'd like to feel you touch me there again, sweet Cassie," he murmured huskily. "But I can wait until we're alone and you attack me again."

Cassidy reared back, sucking her breath in for an outraged retort.

"Cass! Cassidy, ditch the earrings!"

"Wha—what?" Flustered, she stared into the brilliant lights, trying to discern who had spoken.

"The earrings!" Mike hissed, tapping his headphones. "Dick says they're flaring in the lights! Quick—six seconds!"

"Oh hell!" Cassidy snatched off the silver earrings, looking around desperately for a place to put them. Wilde calmly reached across and took them from her hand and, just as Mike counted down the last two seconds, slipped them into his jeans pocket.

"Don't worry, darling," he murmured with a wicked smile. "You can come and get them any time."

"Why, you—"

"You're on!"

Instinct turned her toward the right camera, smile in place. "Hello again," she said warmly. "Last night I promised to bring you the author of one of the most sensational and controversial books in years. *Wilde About Women: Things Your Father Never Taught You* has become the new bible among men who want to know what modern women really want in the bedroom—and the target of feminists across the land. But love it or hate it, one thing's certain: you can't ignore it. And I'm delighted to have the man responsible for creating such controversy right here on *Headliners*, Logan Wilde."

"Believe me, Miss Yorke, the pleasure is all mine." He didn't even bother looking at the camera, and his smile said volumes.

Bristling, Cassidy managed to keep her pleasant smile in place. "Mr. Wilde," she said with deceptive charm, "feminists charge that your book is not only anachronistic in its attitude toward women, but potentially harmful by perpetuating the myth that when a woman says 'no' she's really saying 'yes.' What do you say to that?"

"I say they haven't read it very carefully, Miss Yorke," Wilde replied, managing to put just enough emphasis on her name to remind her that he'd not forgotten her gibe. "My book's about lovemaking. And making love is not a solitary enterprise. It requires, as I'm certain you know, two people—both eager and enthusiastic, both giving and sharing. So, by definition, 'making love' means that both partners are consenting and willing participants."

"But you don't deny that you offer suggestions on how to wear down a woman's resistance?"

"I don't deny that I give suggestions on how a man can become a more proficient lover. If the fact that he's good at what he does encourages a woman to say 'yes,' then I'd say they're both benefiting, wouldn't you?"

"I'd call it seduction, plain and simple."

Wilde's mouth curved in a speculative smile. "Have you got something against seduction, Miss Yorke?"

Cassidy held her temper. "When it's done simply to satisfy one partner's immediate needs, yes."

"Ah," Wilde replied with a quiet laugh, "but that's the whole point, Miss Yorke. Done properly, seduction is a mutual affair. One-sided seduction isn't only unprincipled, it's spectacularly unsatisfying. Unless a man's looking for nothing more rewarding than an anonymous midnight encounter, of course. But then he'd hardly be reading my book, would he?"

"I'm sure I wouldn't know," Cassidy said icily. "The men I date aren't into seduction by any name."

"My condolences," Wilde drawled. "Maybe it's time you went out with a man who knows how to—"

"And love?" Cassidy put in quickly. "Your books seem more concerned with the mechanics of lovemaking than in the emotional aspects of a relationship. Are you really suggesting that if a man has enough technical virtuosity in bed he needn't concern himself with things like mutual respect and commitment?"

"Nothing will ever replace love," Wilde assured her with a smile. "But a bit of technical virtuosity certainly never hurt a relationship. Knowing how to make love well, knowing how to please each other, can only enhance what a man and woman have between them, wouldn't you agree?"

Wilde shifted so he was facing her more fully, managing to arrange his long legs so they held hers trapped against the sofa. It was so subtly done that Cassidy suspected that no one else even realized what he'd done. Certainly it wouldn't be obvious to either the camera or the floor crew. But there was no doubt at all that he'd done it deliberately. As he increased the pressure of his calf against hers, he smiled innocently at her, well aware there was absolutely nothing she could do but smile back.

"Mr. Wilde, isn't this just a joke with you?" she asked through gritted teeth. "I mean, you can't possibly be serious about any of it, can you?"

"Oh, I'm very serious about it, Miss Yorke." Wilde shifted again so his entire calf pressed against hers. He draped his arm casually along the back of the sofa and let his hand drop as though by accident to brush the side of Cassidy's bare neck. She jumped as though electrocuted and Wilde smiled, a glint of devilry sparking in those impudent blue eyes. "I never start anything that I'm not deadly serious about."

"And your books?" Cassidy managed to get out. His fingertips were resting on her shoulder, so lightly, so casually, that no one watching would even realize he was touching her. But as far as Cassidy was concerned, that feather touch was like fire, and there was absolutely nothing she could do about it. Legs pinned between his and the sofa, she couldn't even move away from him. She looked frantically at Mike. Unaware that anything unusual was going on, he smiled and held up three fingers. Three minutes until a commercial break! "I mean, do you intend to write another one, or—?" She froze as he draped his other hand across his knee so his fingers rested lightly on her leg just below the hem of her skirt. Television veteran that he was, he'd done it when he knew the camera would be on her in a tight close-up, hiding his move from the audience while recording her every reaction in vivid detail. Her own knee was between his hand and the camera, effectively shielding it from view. Lightly, he started stroking her thigh with his fingertip.

"That depends on a number of things," he replied helpfully, smiling as he watched her fight to maintain control. "Actually, I was thinking of aiming my next book at women."

"Women?" Cassidy flinched as he ran that mischievous finger slowly back and forth just under the hem of her skirt. "Just what—what could you possibly have to say to women?"

"I'd tell them how to make love to their men," he replied in honeyed tones, his finger tracing a delicate line to her inner knee and back again. It paused there tantalizingly, then started drawing little circles with a light, rhythmic stroke that sent a bolt of electricity through Cassidy. "About the things a man likes. About how—"

"That—that's very interesting," Cassidy stammered, trying desperately to ignore that incredibly erotic caress. From the corner of her eye she saw that Ken had joined Mike, and that they were both staring at her as though wondering what on earth was the matter with her. "But this *is* a family show, Mr. Wilde, so perhaps we'd better not go into details."

Wilde smiled. "Maybe we can discuss it later, Miss Yorke," he suggested amiably.

"I don't think I'm really interested in a how-to manual written by a self-proclaimed professional bachelor," she replied with a control that astonished her. She crossed her legs forcefully, catching him by surprise and ramming the toe of her pump solidly into the back of his left calf. He didn't betray the slightest sign of pain, but Cassidy distinctly heard his breath catch. She smiled sweetly at him. "As a matter of fact, I'm puzzled as to what makes you an expert at all this. Don't you think it's a bit presumptuous, if not arrogant, to make yourself out as the guru of modern day sexual politics?"

"Perhaps I'm just good at what I do," Wilde replied with an engaging smile. Leaning across her lap, ostensibly to reach for a glass of water on the low coffee table, he put his other hand firmly on her thigh, the one hidden from camera and crew. Cassidy stiffened in astonishment, too startled to even move as he ran his palm up her thigh under her skirt when he leaned toward the table again to put the glass back down. Then he relaxed back against the sofa again, his mouth brushed with the faintest of smiles.

His eyes met hers challengingly, as though daring her to succumb to her anger. But as tempting as the urge was, Cassidy restrained herself. *Oh, no!* she seethed silently. *I'll see you in hell before I show even the slightest reaction on-camera.* "How very modest of you," she said pointedly. "I guess I'll have to take your word on it. Now, I'm afraid we have to break for a—"

"Not at all," Wilde put in smoothly. "You don't have to take my word on anything, Miss Yorke. In fact, I'd be more than delighted to submit to a thorough investigation of my abilities any time you wish."

"I hardly think that's necess—"

"Come on now, Miss Yorke," he persisted, eyes glinting with laughter. "You've sat here and publicly doubted my competence. It seems to me that the least you can do is let me prove you wrong."

Both Mike and Ken seemed fascinated. Ken motioned her to ignore the time and continue. Vowing to strangle all three of them, she glared at Wilde. "And just how do you propose that we do that?"

He apppeared to give the matter serious consideration. "Ohhh...how about dinner tomorrow night? It'll give you an opportunity to observe Logan Wilde in his natural habitat and let you judge his competence first-hand."

Two

It was so audacious that Cassidy laughed aloud. "You've forgotten that I've read all your books, and know all the tricks of your trade. I'd hardly be a serious challenge."

"Oh, I suspect you'd be quite a challenge," Wilde replied softly. "And worth every bit of the effort."

The blatant suggestiveness in his voice took Cassidy's breath away. "We have to break for a commercial." Tearing her gaze from his, she looked at the camera, praying she didn't look as rattled as she felt. "We'll be right back for more of Logan Wilde."

It took everyone so much by surprise that the camera stayed on her for nearly a full five seconds before Dick managed to cut over to the commercial tape. The instant the camera prompt light went out, Cassidy was on her feet. She ignored Wilde's quiet laugh as she nearly ran off the set.

"Cass? Cassidy—!" She stopped, breathing heavily, as Ken strode around to face her. "What the hell are you doing out there?" he demanded in a forced whisper. "My God, this is a talk program, not the six o'clock news! You're supposed to be doing a friendly interview with this guy. You're coming across like Harry Reasoner. Lighten up!"

"You don't have to worry about the rest of the show," she hissed, "because I'm not going back out there with that—that maniac!"

"Cassidy, this is live! You can't just quit in the middle of a—"

"Oh, no? Put on a tape, put on Marsh, put on—I don't care what you put on. Just keep that man away from me!"

"Cassidy, for God's sake be reasonable! You call yourself a professional. A professional doesn't walk out in the middle of a live interview because of a personality conflict with her guest. This isn't Oregon, remember. You've got thirty thousand people out there watching you, not three lumberjacks and a forest ranger!"

"Personality conflict?" Cassidy echoed furiously. "That man—"

"I gave you this interview because I thought you could handle it," Ken told her ominously. "I'd hate to think I made a mistake."

Cassidy stared at him, hardly able to believe what she was hearing. And suddenly she realized that no one had the slightest idea of the silent battle she and Wilde had been waging. Unaware of what had been going on, Ken and the others had seen her as the aggressor and Wilde as her unfortunate victim.

"I can handle the interview," she assured him with quiet venom.

He smiled. "That's the girl. And one more thing." Cassidy stiffened, eyes narrowing, but Ken apparently didn't notice. "I want you to go out with Wilde tomorrow night."

Cassidy gaped at him. "You can't be serious! If you think for one minute that—"

"Cassidy, it'll make a fantastic follow-up show!"

"Damn it, Ken, I will not—"

"Think of the ratings, Cass. Every set in transmission range will be locked on KALB the night after next."

"I don't give a hoot about the ratings!" she replied furiously. "I will not—"

"You'd better start giving a hoot about the ratings," Ken reminded her impatiently. "Without them, you don't have a show."

Cassidy stared at him. "Just what are you saying?"

"Nothing that shouldn't always be on the mind of someone planning a career in television. Without ratings, we don't get advertising; without advertising, we have to cancel shows."

Cassidy wheeled away from him, so angry she was nearly shaking. "Air that Taos special, and I'll do it."

"What?" He stared at her, astounded.

"You heard me," she replied calmly. "I can play the game as well as you can, Ken. If you want me to risk life and limb to get you a follow-up show on Logan Wilde, then you can do something for me: okay that Taos show."

She thought for a moment that he was going to explode with anger. Then he suddenly gave a snort of laughter, shaking his head in amusement. "You catch on pretty fast, Cassidy. All right, you've got it. One Taos special. And if Crothers tacks my hide up on the wall, just remember you're responsible."

"The risk is about comparable," she muttered, giving the set a hostile glance. "I just hope I don't regret this."

Wilde was signing autographs when Cassidy made her way back to the set. The stagehands and cameramen were crowding around like neophytes at the foot of the master, apparently deaf to the growing impatience in the floor director's voice as he told them to clear the set. They left reluctantly when Cassidy appeared, clutching their signed copies of Wilde's book like it contained the wisdom of the ages. Which it no doubt did, Cassidy reminded herself, if one was a hopeful young lover looking for a guiding hand through the sexual jungle.

Wilde smiled, looking very relaxed and comfortable, as she walked toward him. "I was beginning to think that you'd left me to finish this interview on my own."

"Don't think it didn't cross my mind," Cassidy assured him, sitting as far from him as she could get and still be on the same set. "We have only ten minutes more of this to get through—then we never have to see each other again. So let's just pretend that we're enjoying ourselves, all right?"

"Are you always this uptight?" he asked casually. "It's a sign of repressed sexual tension. With the right therapy, you should be able to express all that pent-up passion in no time at all."

"You just let me worry about my repressed passions," Cassidy suggested pointedly, securing her microphone. "And so help me," she warned, "if you lay so much as a finger on me during the next ten minutes, I'll deck you right here on live television."

"Another sign of sexual frustration," he murmured with a wicked grin. "When the right man finds the key to your heart, lady, you're going to catch fire."

"Cass!" Mike called urgently. "Move in closer to Logan. We can't get you both in the same shot."

Wilde smiled wolfishly. "You heard the man, Miss Yorke. Come a little closer."

Cassidy slid a scant inch nearer. "I swear that if you so much as—"

"Come on, Cass!" Mike urged with an edge of impatience. "At least get in the same studio with the man!"

Wilde's eyes met hers, suddenly serious. "Let's call a truce, Cass," he offered quietly. "No more games, all right?"

It took Cassidy so by surprise that she stared at him.

Wilde gave her a lopsided smile. "I promise I'll behave. Ten minutes of acting like a jerk is long enough for even me."

This can't be the same Logan Wilde! Cassidy thought in astonishment. She edged slightly nearer, watching him mistrustfully. "I don't know what you're—" Mike's yelp of warning coincided with the scarlet flare of a camera indicator and Cassidy, without missing a beat, turned smoothly toward Camera One. "Hello again. For those of you who have just tuned in, we're talking with author Logan Wilde this evening. His three best-selling books are on the table in front of me. It's impossible to pick up a major newspaper or magazine these days without seeing Mr. Wilde's column, 'Wilde About Loving: The Modern Man's Guide to the Modern Woman.'" She looked at her guest. "Mr. Wilde, why do you think you're so popular?"

"Fear."

Now what, she wondered with an inward groan. First a complete change of character, now this. She'd expected something about repressed sexual tension or the like, and here he was leading her off into unknown territory. "Fear?" she asked cautiously. "Fear of what?"

"Fear of whom," he corrected with a smile. "Women, Miss Yorke. And I see I've surprised you."

"You might say that," Cassidy replied dryly. *And you're a damned liar,* her eyes added. *You've never been afraid of a woman—or anything else, for that matter—in your entire life.* "And what is it about us that frightens you so badly, Mr. Wilde?"

"We're afraid of being hurt." He said it so quietly, so seriously, that Cassidy found herself almost believing him. He smiled, his blue eyes oddly wistful. "You women are changing, and you're demanding more from your men. We put our hearts and our egos on the line every time we initiate or commit to a relationship."

Again, his seriousness caught Cassidy unprepared. She looked at him for an uncertain moment, wondering where this was leading, still not trusting him.

"There are a lot of men out there tired of playing the roles society has given them. They're seeking new answers to old questions. I'm just trying to help out."

It was all a little too glib, Cassidy decided. A little too easy and well-rehearsed: the words themselves, the slight frown, the intent gaze. Surely he didn't think she would fall for this! "How lucky we all are," she offered drolly, "that Logan Wilde appeared when he did to give us the answers."

Wilde's reaction wasn't what she expected. He winced and for a fleeting instant—just a heartbeat of time—what Cassidy could have sworn was bitterness darkened his unsmiling eyes. "Yes," he said in a little more than a whisper. "Yes, I guess we are."

For some unfathomable reason, Cassidy regretted her sarcasm. But even as she was contemplating his odd reaction, Wilde's mood changed. He leaned well back and set one expensively shod foot on the edge of the coffee table. "And speaking of answers, Miss Yorke, I'm still waiting for yours."

Just what are you up to, she demanded silently, every instinct suddenly alert. He smiled in reply, a dangerous little smile that set off every warning bell in Cassidy's being. She stared at him. It was as though a switch had been pulled. Suddenly the serious man, the slightly vulnerable man, was gone and in his place was the first Logan Wilde she'd met, the obnoxious playboy whose every word was a challenge, every gesture a come-on.

She contemplated leaving his question simply hanging there. But Wilde wouldn't be that easily outwitted. "An answer to what?" she asked blandly, smiling in spite of being able to think of nothing but wholesale murder. *Truce, my foot!*

"About dinner tomorrow night," he replied in a husky purr that probably melted half the female hearts in Albuquerque. "You can hardly turn me down, you know. Not when I've asked you out in front of thirty thousand people."

"You don't think so?" she suggested coolly, trying to ignore Ken Vaughn. He was standing beside Mike, hands on hips, staring intently at her. How dare he put her in a predicament like this!

"Well, Cass—excuse me, Miss Yorke—you're not going to break my heart right here on public television, are you? Think of my reputation."

"That's *exactly* what I'm thinking about," Cassidy shot back, eliciting a snort of appreciative laughter from one of the crew. Damn it, what was the matter with her? She was good at this—too good to let a man like Logan Wilde make a fool out of her at her own game. She finally eased her breath between her teeth, realizing she didn't really have a choice. "All right," she said offhandedly, "just for the sake of my viewers, who are undoubtedly dying to know what it's like to date the infamous Logan Wilde, I'll have dinner with you."

Wilde laughed softly. "I promise to make it a night to remember, Miss Yorke," he murmured with a slow, anticipatory smile that made Cassidy wonder if she wouldn't be wiser to resign from KALB on the spot and go back to reporting the weather in Oregon.

She took a deep breath and unlocked her gaze from Wilde's. "Now, for those many viewers who have no interest whatsoever in my social life, let's get on with my next question."

It was a good thing, Cassidy decided nearly an hour later, that KALB put all her shows on tape. Because if she lived to be a hundred she would never be able to remember those last few minutes on-air with Wilde. She had no idea of what she'd asked him, and even less of what he'd replied. The only thing that she was certain of was that it was over.

She dropped into the big armchair in the tiny dressing room she shared with Marsh, feeling utterly drained. What on earth had happened out there? She had lost control of the interview before they had even gone on the air and had never regained it. That had never happened before. Oh, she'd had her share of difficult interviews: the aspiring young nightclub singer who'd flung off her raincoat to happily reveal that she was stark naked; the famous Broadway actor, on tour, who had stumbled offstage and onto KALB cameras so drunk he could scarcely stand; the young woman teaching a natural childbirth class who had gone into labor five minutes into the interview. But she'd handled those crises, and others, with a grace and quick-witted skill that had earned her the respect of the entire station. Even Marsh had once called her "the co-host I'd most want beside me when things go wrong," which, from an egoist like Marsh, was no small accolade. And yet Logan Wilde had led her in circles.

Frowning, Cassidy picked up her hairbrush and turned toward the dressing table. Her own reflection looked back at her, grass-green eyes still snapping with anger, heavy mane of hair tumbling around her face and shoulders. She stared at it for a moment, then pulled the brush through the chestnut tangles. She smiled as she smoothed her hair back from her face and pinned it into a knot at her nape. As always, it gave her a feeling of rebellion, of quiet defiance against KALB and the executives who seemed more interested in sex appeal than brains. It was Ken who had told her to wear her hair loose. "The audience doesn't want you looking like a bank president," he'd said ten months ago. "They want you soft and pretty and sexy. And that gorgeous hair of yours is sexy as hell."

Cassidy sighed as she put her hairbrush away. It was strange, but before she came to KALB she'd never given her looks much thought. She had certainly never thought of herself as sexy. The idea still made her smile. Blondes were sexy, not chestnut-haired brunettes with nondescript colored eyes that were brown one moment and hunter-green the next. Besides, she was too short to be sexy. And too small breasted. She eyed her reflection thoughtfully. One thing was certain: she certainly wasn't Wilde's type of woman. A glance at any newspaper showed that he preferred tall, generously endowed blondes with legs that went on forever.

A tap at the door made her glance up. Ken walked in, grinning with satisfaction. "That was great, Cass. Fantastic! What a gimmick!"

"It's silly and...cheap." Cassidy met his eyes in the dressing table mirror. "I'm terrified that some programming wizard up on the fifth floor's going to come up with an idea for a great new show called *Cassidy Yorke and Her Date-of-the-Week*. With live camera crew and all."

Ken laughed. "Maybe I'll mention it to them."

"Don't bother." Cassidy stood up and picked up her coat. "We had a deal, remember—Logan Wilde for my Taos show."

"You'll get your Taos show. Just bring me a story on Wilde."

"I don't like all this, Ken."

He leaned back against the dressing table, arms crossed. "This is how the game's played, Cass."

Cassidy paused by the door, looking around at him. "This is the last time, Ken," she said softly. "I'll play the game your way this time, but don't ever do this to me again."

"Threats, Cass?" he asked with a raised eyebrow.

"I grew up with three older brothers. One thing it taught me was that if you let someone bully you once, they'll keep on bullying you until you start fighting back." She pulled the door open. "Good night, Ken. And don't forget that I'm not going to be at the planning meeting tomorrow morning. I'm taking a film crew out to Alamgordo for my show on UFOs."

"Yeah." He nodded, frowning thoughtfully. "Just don't be late for your date with Wilde. Where is he picking you up?"

"Here, right after the show tomorrow night."

"Here?" Ken gave her a look of disbelief. "This is a date, not a meeting with your stockbroker! A drink at your apartment, then—"

"I'm not letting that man within a country mile of my apartment," she told him darkly. "As far as I'm concerned, this is just another KALB assignment."

Cassidy repeated the words to herself firmly a few minutes later as she made her way out to the parking lot. Logan Wilde had asked her out because it made good publicity, and she had accepted because promotional gimmicks were part of the job. And that, she added as she wheeled her little red MGB out into traffic, was all there was to it.

Except that wasn't all there was to it. And by the following evening, Cassidy had stopped trying to pretend that it was. She leaned toward the *Headliners* dressing room mirror to run a line of brown eyeshadow carefully along her lashes. She smudged it with her fingertip, then drew back to see the results. Then, deliberately, she met her own gaze in the mirror. Because if this really *is* just another assignment, she taunted her reflection, why are you going to this much trouble? She stood back and eyed the new dress critically. She had bought it on impulse that afternoon, an electric-blue silk cocktail dress with a loose fitting camisole top and gathered skirt. There was no denying that it looked spectacular, she decided, doing a slow pirouette in front of the full-length mirror. The gossamer-thin spaghetti straps, crossed in the back, looked like strings of sapphires against her tan, and the skirt followed her every movement sensuously.

Not exactly the kind of garb she usually chose for "just another assignment"! Why don't you admit that you're fascinated with the man and get it over with, she asked herself bluntly. *He got to you yesterday. Like it or not, you're obviously no more immune to that devastating charm and magical sex appeal than any other woman.*

"He's here!" Assistant producer Jeri Martell burst in, wide-eyed with awe. "Cassidy, he's really here!"

"Okay, Jeri, thanks. I'll be right there." Cassidy gave her reflection one last inspection. She had swept her hair up into a sleek coil above her left ear, adding an exotic enameled haircomb trimmed with peacock feathers. Bold square-cut earrings of blue crystal added the finishing touch.

"He's so gorgeous!" Jeri groaned. "He looks at me with those fantastic blue eyes and I just melt."

"Book One, Chapter Five: 'The Basics of Flirting.' Or, how to reduce a woman to jelly with one smoldering glance. It's all by the book, Jeri."

"He can lead me through all three books, chapter and verse, any time. Do you have any idea how many women would kill to trade places with you tonight?"

"Just part of the job," Cassidy reminded her.

"But somebody's got to do it, right? What courage! What intrepid valor!" She sighed yearningly. "I wish someone would ask me to make a sacrifice like this!"

Wilde was standing by the set talking with Ken and Marsh. To Cassidy's surprise, he was casually dressed in a pair of tan linen slacks and a cream-colored cashmere sweater, the sleeves pushed up carelessly to bare his tanned forearms. He glanced up, doing a double take worthy of any comedy routine to stare at her as she walked toward them.

Marsh glanced around curiously, his eyes widening when he saw her. "Wow!" he blurted. "You're always gorgeous, Cassidy, but tonight you've outdone yourself!"

Cassidy gave a merry laugh. "And you're always an outrageous flirt, Marsh Wheeler, but thank you anyway." She looked up at Wilde, still laughing, and held out her hand. "Hello again. I think Marsh has been reading your books on the sly. That line had Logan Wilde written all over it."

Even prepared for it, Cassidy felt as though she'd been hit with a tidal wave when those bottomless blue eyes locked with hers. He smiled that slow, heart melting smile as his fingers folded around hers. "The gentleman said it all, Miss Yorke. Anything I could add would be purely anticlimactic."

"This is all very heady, but we're starting to draw a crowd. And unless you want to spend the evening signing autographs..."

"That," Wilde assured her, "is most definitely not how I want to spend the evening." It was perfectly on-cue, with exactly the right amount of eye contact and husky suggestiveness in his voice to make Cassidy's pulse give a silly little leap before she could remind herself that it was all a game. Letting her fingers slide through his in a lingering caress, he shook hands with Ken and Marsh, then settled his hand on Cassidy's waist and escorted her toward the door. "Let's get out of here," he said softly. "Before that producer of yours decides to send a camera crew out after us."

Cassidy gave a sputter of laughter. "I hope you made reservations under a false name," she teased, only half joking. "If you didn't, he'll have every potted palm in the restaurant bristling with cameras and long-range mikes."

Wilde held the studio door open. "I can guarantee he won't find us tonight," he assured her. "I'm taking *you* out tonight, Miss Yorke, not KALB Television and half of Albuquerque."

Cassidy said nothing, thinking of the tiny tape recorder in her handbag with something suspiciously like guilt. A ghost-gray Ferrari crouched at the curb and as Wilde walked her toward it, Cassidy smiled. "Nice car. But then again, what else would Logan Wilde drive?"

Wilde's mouth quirked in a sardonic smile. He pulled the car door open and helped her in. "Image, Miss Yorke. All part of the packaging."

For an instant, Cassidy could have sworn that she heard the same trace of bitterness in Wilde's voice that she had detected during their interview. She glanced at him curiously as he slid into the car beside her. "You know, you still haven't told me where we're going."

"Do you like paella? And sweet red wine?"

"Sounds delicious."

He gave her an amused glance. "Then trust me."

Trust me! Cassidy resisted the urge to scream and instead relaxed back into the lush leather seat with an inward sigh. If she'd heard that phrase once in the past ten months, she'd heard it a hundred times. It was Ken Vaughn's favorite: *trust me,* he would say. *I'll get you the format changes you want, Cass, I swear it! Trust me.* She wondered if Logan Wilde's directive would be equally unworthy of her faith.

The Ferrari was already purring to a stop by the time Cassidy realized that Wilde had pulled in. She gave the gleaming glass tower soaring above them a puzzled glance and turned to ask Wilde where they were, but he was already half out of the car. A uniformed valet opened her door and she slid out as Wilde came around the car. Handing his keys to the valet, he took her arm and led her up the wide marble steps to where the doorman was already holding open the heavy glass door. He smiled and greeted Wilde by name, and it wasn't until they were in the luxuriously furnished lobby that Cassidy realized what was going on.

She gave Wilde a shrewd look. "It's funny," she reflected dryly, "but when you asked me out to dinner, I don't remember your mentioning that it was going to be in your apartment."

Wilde looked down at her. "I promised to take you somewhere private and quiet," he reminded her. "And I always deliver what I promise, Miss Yorke."

"I'll keep that in mind." She forced herself to hold the brazen stare nonchalantly. *My God, what nerve!*

"We could always go somewhere else, somewhere more public, if you're afraid to be alone with me."

He was good, Cassidy had to admit. He knew every move of the game. "Don't flatter yourself," she said with a tolerant smile as she started to walk toward the elevators. "I've faced worse hazards for a story. And I've never encountered a situation—or a man—yet that I haven't been able to handle." She looked at him coolly as he caught up to her. "And I doubt, Mr. Wilde, that you're an exception."

Wilde gave a snort of surprised laughter. "No, I'll bet you haven't. But then, most men are intimidated by bright, independent women." He reached past her to hold the elevator door open, smiling down at her. "But in that, Miss Yorke, I am very much an exception."

The elevator door whispered closed and Cassidy had a moment of panicky doubt. What in God's name was she doing here? No story was worth this. She should have stood her ground with Ken instead of buckling under at the first subtle threat. Because this entire evening was turning into more than she'd bargained for. No matter how sophisticated and worldly she pretended to be, Cassidy Yorke was still a country kid from small town Oregon, slightly naive and hopelessly old-fashioned. Logan Wilde didn't know that, of course. He saw the Cassidy Yorke everyone saw and undoubtedly believed the lie. She slid him an uneasy glance and found him watching her, mouth curved in a small smile as though he knew exactly what she was thinking.

The elevator opened onto a small lobby filled with lush greenery. Overhead, a skylight glowed with stars. Wilde approached the only door and slid a plastic identification card into the slot. There was a pause, a click, and the door glided open soundlessly.

Penthouse suite. What else, Cassidy thought silently. Logan Wilde would hardly live like mortal men. She stepped into the huge entrance, eyes widening. The marble floor gleamed like black ice in the soft illumination radiating from hidden niches in the mirrored ceiling. The walls were paneled with the same vast unbroken sheets of smoke-gray mirrors and as Wilde stepped beside her their reflections seemed to shift and multiply endlessly. Silently, she followed as he led her down a wide corridor lined with framed photographic prints and paintings: Edward Weston, a signed print of Ansel Adams' famous Hernandez moonrise shot, a couple of rare Georgia O'Keeffe oils.

"Good Lord!" Cassidy whispered involuntarily as they walked down three curved carpeted stairs into the living room.

Dimly lit, it seemed to go forever. Lush charcoal-gray carpeting blended with the dark gray and black reflective wallpaper. Panels of mirrors doubled everything, then doubled it again, catching a mosaic of reflections from floor and ceiling and walls. It took Cassidy a moment to realize that two solid walls were glass and that she was staring not at glittering shards of reflected light, but at city lights. A curved sofa of luxurious cream leather sat to one side, offset by a scattering of modular leather chairs and low glass tables. It was everything Logan Wilde's apartment should have been, right down to the life-sized bronze nude standing on a low black acrylic base in the angle where the two walls of glass met.

"How about an aperitif?"

"All right." Cassidy walked across to the windows and gazed out silently for several minutes. It was a breathtaking view of the city, edged by blackness in the distance. The sky glowed with stars and pale light from the rising moon. Laughing in delight, she turned around. "This is the most fantastic—" She blinked in surprise. Wilde was gone.

"I'm in here," came his voice from a corridor to her left. "Come on down."

Tentatively, Cassidy started down the corridor. Doors ran off to left and right, one leading to what looked like a small bedroom, the other to an office or den. Wilde was in neither. The double doors at the end of the corridor were open. Cassidy could hear a shower running somewhere and, unabashedly curious to see if this infamous room that played such a part in his books was anything at all as she had imagined, she walked up three shallow stairs and into Wilde's bedroom.

A huge bed sat in a mirrored alcove to one side, draped with black fur. Low pieces of black laquered furniture sat here and there, gleaming like polished ebony in the subdued lighting. A life-sized bronze wolfhound stared curiously at her from beside the black marble fireplace. Opposite the bed, three broad, curving steps led down to a massive sunken octagonal whirlpool tub set in a niche of floor-to-ceiling windows overlooking the city. The narrow space between the tub and the curved sweep of glass was filled with a lush jungle of tropical plants, their mirrored containers glittering with stray reflections. The view, as from the living room, was spectacular. The city spread out below like a jeweled carpet, and Cassidy realized it would be possible to relax here in total privacy, invisible to the inhabitants far below. Two martini glasses and a silver shaker sat on the foot-wide border of black marble that ran the circumference of the tub. A plush burgundy velour robe lay beside the glasses.

"Hi." Cassidy wheeled around as Wilde padded out of the adjoining bathroom, wearing only a loosely belted velour robe that matched the one by the tub. He was barefoot and his hair was slightly tousled and damply gleaming. "I thought we'd have our drinks in the tub. Make yourself comfortable while I play chef for a minute or two. I'll be right back."

Three

Cassidy looked at the tub. The man certainly didn't waste any time! She felt a blush graze her cheeks and turned her face resolutely away, hoping he hadn't seen it. She was out of her depth here, way, way out of her depth. She had been worrying on and off about this dinner date all day, trying to anticipate every move he would make, formulating her countermoves, rehearsing every step of the evening right down to the good-night kiss at her apartment door. But even her most vivid imaginings hadn't included a nude frolic in his whirlpool!

Fighting for time, she wandered toward the windows, and pretended to admire the view. She took a deep breath and looked around at Wilde. "It sounds marvelous," she said with what she hoped sounded like honest regret. "But I didn't bring my swimsuit."

"That," he drawled, "is the whole idea." His eyes held hers boldly for a moment, then he gave a soft laugh. "I didn't take you for a prude."

The challenge came through loud and very clear. Prude, she thought angrily. *You're damned right!* "Thanks," she said evenly, strolling back toward the door, "but I think I'll pass."

The living room was dark and still. Cassidy walked across to the sweeping wall of glass overlooking the city and stared down at the glowing lights. You're certainly handling the evening so far with your usual wit and sophistication, she told herself disgustedly. *One smooth move by the master himself, and you bolt like a startled deer. He's probably in there right now scratching your name out of his little black book.*

She sighed, realizing that the hollow feeling in her stomach wasn't the anger she expected, but savage disappointment. She'd almost believed him, she thought despairingly. She had almost decided that the movie idol looks, smooth words and aggressive sexuality were simply part of the put-on, part of the role he played to market the books. And suddenly, for no reason at all, she felt like crying.

Just then, Cassidy realized that Wilde had come up silently behind her. She stiffened slightly as his eyes met hers in the darkened glass. "I'm sorry," he said very quietly. "I didn't mean to embarrass or offend you."

It took her by surprise. She'd expected anger, derision, sarcasm—anything but the weary despair she saw in his eyes. "You didn't," she said quietly. She turned around. He'd changed into a pair of blue jeans and a loose-fitting white T-shirt with a University of Mexico insignia printed on it. She found herself smiling, wondering if it was legitimate or if he'd picked it up at the same souvenir shop where she had bought hers. "I'm sorry for being such a wet blanket and spoiling your evening. I should have warned you that I'm still just an Oregon country kid at heart. If I leave right now you can still salvage the evening. There must be a thousand women out there who'd love to sip martinis in your whirlpool. It's a shame to waste them."

He stared at her for a silent moment, his face curiously shadowed and bleak. "I don't suppose there's a chance in hell I can persuade that Oregon country kid to stay, is there?" He smiled wearily. "I'd like to back up and start this evening all over, Cassidy. And I'd still like to take you out to dinner—to a real restaurant, this time."

Not for the first time since meeting this enigmatic, aggravating man, Cassidy found herself at a loss for words. It's a trick, something whispered, more of the seductive charm, the smooth manipulation. Part of her wanted to laugh in his face and walk out, but another part of her wanted to stay. She wanted to believe that the contrite wistfulness in his eyes was real. She hesitated, torn. Then, impulsively, she smiled. "You mentioned something about paella and sweet red wine, didn't you? Were you serious, or was it merely a plot to get me up here and into your whirlpool?"

It was Wilde's turn to look startled. Then he gave a soft laugh, shaking his head. "You are some kind of woman. And yes, I was serious about the paella and wine. Does this mean you'll stay?"

"As long as we stay on dry land."

Wilde grinned engagingly. "That's fine by me. I hate drinking martinis in that damned whirlpool anyway. The steam dilutes the vermouth, and the olives clog the recirc pump something crazy!"

Cassidy gave a burst of laughter. "Then why on earth go through all . . . that?" She gestured toward the bedroom.

His smile turned slightly bitter. "Most women seem to expect it. Logan Wilde has a reputation to maintain, remember."

Cassidy nodded slowly, holding his gaze. "Well, I don't like that Logan Wilde very much. I much prefer the man who's promised me paella and wine."

"Good. What do you say," he murmured, "to forgetting about Logan Wilde altogether? Let's pretend that he's somewhere else tonight, doing whatever it is that he does best, while you and I get to know each other?"

Cassidy realized with a little thrill of delicious anticipation that he was going to kiss her. Part of her wanted to do what she would normally do in a situation like this—move out of reach with a minimum of fuss, smiling to alleviate any bruised feelings while making it very clear that she wasn't interested. But another part of her, a part she didn't even recognize, wanted very badly to stay right there. Professional curiosity, she told herself dazedly, watching his mouth near. Just professional curiosity...

His kiss was much more intimate than the moment called for, but Cassidy was neither shocked nor even surprised when she felt the first probing touch of his tongue. It met her tentative response with gentle encouragement and to Cassidy's surprise she found herself kissing him back with a totally uncharacteristic lack of restraint. When he finally lifted his mouth from hers, her breathing was decidedly unsteady.

"I'd like to continue this discussion a little later," he murmured with a husky catch in his voice. "But in the meantime, why don't you rescue that shaker of martinis while I start proving that I can do more than talk a good line?"

Wilde was making a dressing for the salad when Cassidy came back with the shaker and glasses. He handled the bewildering array of oils and flavored vinegars and herbs with the casual competence of someone who knows what he's doing, and Cassidy, her own cooking skills shaky at best, prudently decided to stay out of the way. She filled the glasses and set one beside him, then took the other and walked around to the other side of the breakfast island and perched on one of the high leather stools.

She watched him, fascinated. "You're pretty good at that."

He grinned companionably at her. "Basic survival skills as demonstrated by modern urban man, Miss Yorke—tarragon vinegar, olive oil, a pinch or two of this, a sprinkle of that. You'd never know it to look at me, but I'm a damned good cook."

"You're right, I wouldn't," Cassidy shot back. "Your books don't exactly indicate an interest in gourmet cooking, apart from a couple of interesting, if unlikely, things that can be done with whipped cream."

"You've really done your homework, haven't you Cass? Whoops, I mean Miss Yorke."

"I always research my guests thoroughly, Mr. Wilde. And don't you think you've rubbed my nose in that enough by now? It's Cassidy. Or Cass."

"Dare I hope this slight thaw in relations indicates we may have a full-scale truce before the evening's out?"

"Perhaps a temporary cessation of hostilities, anyway."

"Good!" Wilde sounded honestly relieved. "God, you're proper hell on wheels when that camera light goes red, aren't you? After the show I checked to see if any of the knife wounds were visible."

"You held your own with no problem," Cassidy reminded him dryly. "Do you always behave like that on-camera?"

"Only when I'm trying to protect my hide. I dropped in expecting a typical friendly fireside chat and found myself under seige."

"Hah! You got off easy."

"Easy? I've sat through tax audits that were easier!"

Cassidy grinned. "You were lucky that the powers that be won't let me run that show as it should be run, or I'd really have put the heat on."

"Having a few artistic differences with your producers?" Wilde gave her a curious glance, shaking the cruet of dressing vigorously.

Cassidy's smile faded and she tapped the rim of her glass with her fingertip. "Let's just say a difference of opinion about the direction the show's taking."

"Serious?"

"From my viewpoint, or theirs?" Then she gave a quiet laugh. "Just call it a clash of expectations. When I came out here from Oregon, I thought I was going to be doing a serious show. Not quite *60 Minutes*, granted, but something a little meatier than *Cassidy's Corner.* I didn't realize all they wanted was fluff."

"A pretty face to keep the ratings up," Wilde corrected with surprising insight. "Did you have your own show in Oregon?"

Cassidy gave a sputter of laughter. "Hardly. I was part of the local news team."

"Really?" Wilde looked interested. He leaned one hip against the counter and picked up his drink. "If that brief taste of Cassidy Yorke I had last night was any example of your on-camera reporting skills, you must have done one hell of a job."

Cassidy looked at him mischievously over the rim of her glass. "I just said I was part of the news team. I didn't say which part. As a matter of fact, I was 'Weather Woman.'"

"'Weather *what*'?" Wilde demanded, staring at her as though not believing what he'd heard.

Cassidy smiled wearily. "Oh, it started out legitimately enough, I guess. It's not unusual for a station to put new talent on the weather board to get them used to working on-camera. I wasn't very happy with it—I'd had plenty of camera experience during college—but I went along with it because I wanted the job. It was supposed to be just temporary until they could fit me into one of the field reporting teams. But for some reason I was a big hit. It even caught the programming geniuses by surprise." She gave her head a disgusted shake. "But it didn't take them long to catch on and to play the ratings for all they were worth. I started out seriously enough in sedate little business suits, and the next thing I knew I was 'Weather Woman,' complete with a 'weather wand' to point to cold fronts, trading one-liners with the news staff." She blushed slightly, remembering. "Believe it or not, it took me nearly six months to realize they had no intention of putting me on real news as long as the weather ratings held up."

"Sometimes success can be its own worst punishment."

"So I discovered." Cassidy stared into her martini thoughtfully.

"Why do you stay?"

The question was so matter-of-fact that it left Cassidy momentarily nonplussed. "I keep asking myself the same question," she finally admitted. "More often during the last couple of weeks. A major Seattle station's offered me a position as news anchor in their prime-time slot, and—" She stopped dead. "Damn!" she breathed in annoyance. "I have no idea why I'm telling you this. No one else even knows about it yet." Frowning, she gave her martini a dark look. "I think I've had enough of this. I don't usually babble on like this to perfect strangers."

"Hardly perfect," he answered, eyes locked with hers. "And I'd like to think that before this evening's over we're going to be anything but strangers." Cassidy's pulse gave an irrational leap as he put both elbows on the counter separating them and leaned toward her, taking the glass from her hand and setting it aside. He took her hand in his and turned it over, starting to kiss the inside of her wrist. "You're a bright, beautiful and appealing woman, Cassidy Yorke. And I'm discovering a special weakness where you're concerned."

A wave of dizziness washed through Cassidy as his tongue moved leisurely on her wrist, tracing a warm, damp spiral into her palm. "I didn't think Logan Wilde had a weakness of any sort," she countered breathlessly. "Especially where women are concerned."

"Ordinarily, no. But you," he murmured, kissing each of her knuckles in turn, "are a whole different story." Then, before Cassidy could manage a dazed reply, he straightened, letting her fingers slide through his. "Why don't you bring your drink into the dining room while I prove that my culinary virtuosity extends beyond a flair for whipped cream."

Wilde's promise was more than an idle boast. The salad was delicious, an imaginative mix of artichoke hearts and crisp green vegetables marinated in a tart dressing. The paella was even better. It was made in the traditional Spanish manner with rice, chicken and highly spiced chorizo sausages, seasoned with garlic and saffron and garnished with mussels and shrimp. Wilde served it with hot crusty bread and plenty of Spanish wine and then brought out a cool raspberry mousse for dessert.

As a matter of fact, Cassidy found herself thinking hours later, it had all been utterly perfect. Curled up on the vast semicircular sweep of the sofa, she watched Wilde as he toyed with an array of stereo components tucked unobtrusively in the built-in wall unit. Soft music washed through the room, subtle and romantic, and Cassidy took a sip of her wine to hide her smile. More perfection in an already perfect evening. He was playing it by the book, she thought—his book. Next, he would ask her to dance, then would come the embrace, the kiss...

She smiled again, too relaxed and comfortable to even mind that all this perfection was just part of an elaborate game, or that she was one of many with whom it had been played. It was so easy to just pretend that this evening was as special to him as it was to her, that *she* was special, and to simply enjoy the evening. For there was no denying, she mused lazily, that there was a good deal to be enjoyed—the meal, the wine, the music, Logan Wilde. Perhaps, especially, Logan Wilde.

There was magic about him, she'd decided hours ago. How else to explain that she'd been on the verge of murdering the man on live television last night, and tonight she was halfway in love with him? It wasn't just his good looks and relaxed charm that had captivated her. Nor the easy way he had of making her laugh. Not even the way he turned every megawatt of those phenomenal blue eyes on her and made her feel that she was the most beautiful, clever and wondrously desirable woman in the entire universe. No, she decided comfortably, it had to be magic.

It was as though a spell had been cast over the evening. Wilde was a marvelous conversationalist. There didn't seem to be anything he couldn't discuss knowledgeably, few books he hadn't read, few things he hadn't done or places he hadn't been. And the odd part of it all, she had to admit, was that it didn't seem to be an act. In fact, watching his animated expression while he was describing a recent trip through the game preserves of Kenya, she suddenly had the feeling that Logan Wilde had vanished altogether, leaving behind this fascinating stranger who was quickly stealing her heart.

Which wasn't wise, she reminded herself with a sigh. Because illusions or not, this man *was* Logan Wilde. And Logan Wilde collected hearts like a schoolboy collected butterflies, past trophies forgotten in the heat of the latest chase and capture. She would be pinned to the walls of his memory with a thousand others, just another momentary burst of color in a fading mosaic.

"You're looking very contemplative."

Cassidy looked up, finding Wilde smiling down at her. She gave a quiet laugh. "I'm contemplating the last of my wine. It's very good."

"It's the last of a case I brought back from Barcelona last fall. There's enough for another half glass each."

"No, please." Cassidy held up her hand. "You finish it. One small glass is my limit, and I'm well past that—in fact, you're starting to blur around the edges a bit already."

"There's a cure for that." Smiling, Wilde set his glass aside and reached for her hand. "Come dance with me, Cassidy."

Right on cue! Smiling to herself, she let him pull her to her feet. She stepped into his arms, fitting to him as though she had always belonged there, and they fell into step to the slow, romantic music.

"What's that little smile about?"

"You." She smiled mischievously. "Dinner. Wine. Dancing. If I didn't know better, Mr. Wilde, I'd say you had seduction on your mind."

"I do." Then he gave a quiet laugh and pulled her nearer to him. "Don't look so worried, Cass," he murmured against her ear. "I already told you that I don't believe in one-sided seduction. Whatever happens between us tonight will happen because it's what you want."

Cassidy gave an astonished laugh, pulling back far enough to look up at him. "You really are one of the most amazingly self-satisfied men I've met in years. What on earth gives you the idea there's even the remotest possibility of something 'happening' between us—tonight, or any other night?"

"Just call it a feeling." His gaze held hers with sultry amusement. "Something's already happening between us, Cass. It started last night at KALB. You felt it then, just as I did. And you're still feeling it, just as I am."

"That old black magic?" she speculated with a droll laugh, trying to pretend that she didn't know what he was talking about. But denying it didn't make it any less true; something *was* happening between them. Something more than soft lighting, too much wine and romantic music could account for. But was it honest male-female chemistry, she wondered. Or just more of that lethal Logan Wilde charisma?

"Call it what you like, Cass," he murmured, gaze still locked with hers. "But whatever it is, it's real. Don't try to tell me you're not feeling what I'm feeling."

Would he stop looking at her like that! His indigo gaze was as warmly intimate as a physical caress, and it made her feel dizzy. That, and the heady scent of his cologne, the warmth of the strong male hand resting comfortably on the upper swell of her bottom, the vital masculinity emanating from him. "What I'm feeling is hardly surprising, considering the circumstances,'' she protested with a slightly unsteady laugh. ''You're very good at this, Logan Wilde!''

''Not good enough to get Cassidy Yorke into my bed unless she choses to be there,'' he murmured, his hand pressing her hips ever so gently against him. ''And frankly, I wouldn't want it any other way.''

Her pulse gave a leap. ''Are you admitting that you want to sleep with me?'' she asked lightly, making a joke of it.

''Yes.''

The unapologetic truth took Cassidy's breath away. It wasn't Wilde's blunt honesty that bothered her as much as the fact that she wasn't nearly as outraged by it as she should have been. ''Very direct and to the point,'' she said offhandedly, doubting her feigned calm fooled him any more than her levity had. ''I'll admit that I was expecting something more subtle.''

''Does my honesty bother you?''

''No,'' she lied. ''I'm just surprised that you're not following your own advice. According to the Wilde handbook, only barbarians and disco dilettantes ask a woman point-blank to go to bed with them. Subtlety, I believe you've written, is the name of the game.''

''If I was interested in playing games with you, Cass, I'd have suggested backgammon. And I haven't asked you—point-blank or otherwise—to go to bed with me. You asked a question; I answered it.''

''But you don't deny if the opportunity presented itself, you wouldn't turn it down.''

Wilde's gaze held hers, faintly troubled. ''I'd be lying if I said it wouldn't be tempting,'' he admitted after a moment.

''I thought Logan Wilde advocated snatching opportunity first and indulging in self-examination later.''

The faintest hint of a smile brushed Wilde's strong mouth. ''You're quite a student of Logan Wilde, aren't you? Is there anything I've written that you haven't read?''

"It's part of my job," she replied quietly, suddenly ashamed of baiting him. "I wanted to know you, to figure what makes you tick, before our interview."

"And did you? Figure out what makes me tick, I mean?"

Cassidy looked up at him. His eyes were only inches from hers and she felt something she didn't understand pass between them, some tiny electric charge that had been between them all evening. "I thought I did," she admitted in a whisper. "I thought I had you all figured out, Logan Wilde. But I'm beginning to think I don't really know you at all."

"And I'm beginning to think," he offered softly, "that there's one hell of a lot more to you than I'd expected, too." His mouth dropped gently to hers, warm and malleable and softly inviting.

Cassidy's eyes felt so heavy lidded she let them close as Wilde coaxed her mouth open under his. The silken touch of his tongue against hers made her shiver, and she let her head fall back as Wilde's kiss deepened with a slow, rhythmic intensity. She'd never been so physically aware of a kiss before, so conscious of the feel of a man's mouth moving on hers, of the musky male taste of him, of the hot, slippery silk of his tongue, the rhythmic thrusts as intimate as any lovemaking. Leisurely, he explored every satin part of her mouth with sensuous enjoyment and she wondered dazedly if it was possible to become drunk on a kiss, knowing she tasted as sweetly of wine as he did.

They were still dancing, Wilde's arm holding her firmly against him as they moved slowly to the music. Dimly, Cassidy became aware that his body was responding with increasing urgency to their closeness and the uninhibited eroticism of their kiss. He gently yet deliberately drew her hips against his, his strong hand caressing the curves of her back and bottom through the thin silk of her dress. Finally, slowly, he eased his mouth from hers. Eyes closed, Cassidy rested her forehead against his chest as they moved slowly with the music.

It was a long while later that the music ended. Ignoring it, they continued dancing. After a moment or two, the tape cassette clicked off and Wilde sighed, arms still locked around her. "I think the band went home."

"Sounds like it," Cassidy murmured, some tiny part of her mind wondering if she wouldn't be wise to do the same thing. Every second she stayed increased the risk of falling helplessly under this man's spell. More under his spell, she corrected. She thought of her tape recorder, still in her handbag. She'd taken it out earlier, then had promptly turned it off and tucked it back in her bag. There'd be no follow-up show on Logan Wilde. And frankly, she was glad of it. This evening had turned into something too private, too special, to share with anyone. And her Taos show? She sighed. She would get it aired one day. But honestly, not as payment in some complicated corporate game of Ken's.

Logan's breath was warm against her skin as he kissed the side of her throat. "Could I interest you in a glass of brandy and an espresso?"

"If it's a very large espresso and a very small brandy, unless you want me falling asleep on you."

Logan's palms flattened against her lower back, pressing her against him. "You have no idea," he breathed huskily, "what a tantalizing image that evokes."

Cassidy drew in an unsteady breath, having a sudden and astonishingly vivid idea of exactly the image he had. "You—you were saying something about brandy and coffee?" she whispered a trifle desperately, knowing she should stop this before it got out of hand.

"Is there any way I could sweet-talk you into joining me in the whirlpool?" He ran his mouth along her temple.

Cassidy closed her eyes, trying to get her senses in order. This whole evening had happened too quickly for her to understand any of it, beyond the fact that things were moving much, much too fast.

"What are you wearing under this dress? Besides some pretty spectacular perfume and a tan that seems to go on forever?"

"What—? Oh. A—a bodysuit."

"You mean one of those leotard things you wear while exercising?"

"Sort of."

"It's like a bathing suit, isn't it?"

Seeing what he was getting at, Cassidy frowned. "I guess so," she allowed doubtfully.

"Well, then?" he murmured gently. "How about it, Cass? Brandy in the whirlpool?"

Cassidy swallowed again, looking up at him. "All right," she breathed, scarcely believing she was saying it aloud until she heard her own voice.

Logan's gaze held hers, his eyes warm and smoky. "You go ahead. I'll get the brandy and join you in a minute."

The water was deep and warm and scented faintly of roses. Cassidy rested her head back against the molded edge of the tub, smiling to herself. Yesterday, if anyone had suggested that she would wind up relaxing half-naked in Logan Wilde's whirlpool, she would have laughed him out of the studio. Which only proved, she mused, that nothing was a certainty except her ability to surprise even herself sometimes.

"I'd like to think that smile was on my account," came a soft voice from just beside her.

Cassidy opened her eyes. Logan was kneeling beside her, two brandy snifters of amber liquor in his hand. He held one out to her. She lifted a dripping hand to take it, aware that his curious gaze was perusing the well tanned length of her through the crystalline water. She found herself smiling again, wondering what he'd expected. The truth was that the royal-blue bodysuit, although strapless and cut high on the hip, was considerably more sedate than most bathing suits. But if he was disappointed in it, or in the fact that she had kept it on, he didn't show it. He stood up and pulled the sweatshirt over his head, then unzipped his jeans and slipped out of them.

Unable to help herself, Cassidy slipped him an oblique glance. To her relief, he was wearing a pair of French-cut briefs nearly the same color as her bodysuit which, although daringly cut, provided at least a pretense at modesty. Tanned and fit, he was in perfect physical condition, his chest hard, his stomach and thighs taut and flat. The only flaw in that male perfection was a long surgical scar on the inside of his left knee.

Logan smiled as he caught her looking at it. "Ski accident," he explained, stepping into the water. "I got bushwacked by a tree a couple of winters ago and spent the following eight weeks in plaster."

Cassidy had to laugh. "I think," she teased, "that the idea is to go around them."

"Oh, I tried," he assured her, relaxing into the hot water beside her. He rested one arm behind her head and leaned across her to lift a false tile in the marble border to reveal a control panel. "But this was a very devious tree. It waited until I was nearly by it, then leapt out at me." Smiling, he turned his head to look at her, his face inches from hers. "I didn't have a chance." He leaned down and kissed her lightly on the mouth. "If I promise to watch out for trees, will you come skiing with me this winter?"

Cassidy smiled. "Yes. Although be forewarned—I haven't strapped on a pair of skis since I left Oregon."

"Just like riding a bicycle," he teased, turning his attention back to the control panel. A flick or two of his fingers and the room lighting dimmed slowly until they were sitting in near darkness. The lights of the city below glittered and shimmered on the mirrored planters around them, and suddenly the soft strains of an orchestra wafted around them.

"Impressive, Mr. Wilde. A little flamboyant, perhaps, but definitely impressive."

One corner of Logan's mouth lifted. "This job does have an advantage or two, all right."

"Job?" Cassidy gave a quiet, skeptical laugh. "All the men I know would give ten years of their lives to be Logan Wilde."

"A man can starve on honey and cakes," he muttered almost to himself, frowning slightly.

Cassidy watched him curiously over the rim of her glass. Serpents in Eden? she wondered idly. She nearly asked him what he meant when the whirlpool pump came on with a muted whirr, swirling the water around them in silken jets.

Logan glanced aside, catching her staring at him thoughtfully. Something shadowed his eyes—weariness, perhaps, or sadness. Then it was gone. He smiled. "That all right?"

Don't push it, something told her. Cassidy smiled, relaxing into the water until her shoulders were submerged, head resting on his arm. "Too much so," she murmured, closing her eyes. "It's better than a massage. I might just stay here all night."

"Promises, promises," he murmured huskily. "And I do massages, too, just as further incentive."

"I know." Cassidy smiled without bothering to open her eyes. "You spend an entire chapter in your second book on how to give a personalized massage."

"And the next chapter describing how to properly enjoy what happens after you've followed my instructions," he said quietly close to her ear.

"I must have skipped that chapter," Cassidy lied blithely, remembering every detail of that erotically descriptive chapter with a little shiver. Her vivid memory was intensified by the sensation of Logan's breath on her throat, the pressure of his thigh and hip against hers, and she had to fight the conscious desire to turn toward him and lose herself in the willing embrace she knew she would find.

"I guess that means I'll just have to explain everything as we go along," he offered in a voice that made Cassidy's toes curl. "Step by step."

"Are you always this obliging?"

"You wouldn't believe how obliging I can be," he whispered, touching her earlobe with the tip of his tongue.

Cassidy shivered slightly and turned her face against his. He rubbed his cheek against hers, his freshly shaven skin as smooth as satin, and Cassidy turned her face even more so her mouth was under his. His lips parted obligingly and he brushed them languidly across hers again and again. His tongue touched hers delicately, then he kissed the corner of her mouth and leaned back, taking a sip of his brandy.

Cassidy opened her eyes, feeling dizzy, a little surprised and disappointed that he had stopped kissing her. He smiled down at her. "You never did tell me if you're taking that job in Seattle or not."

She smiled back. "I didn't realize it was that important. Does the rest of the evening depend on my answer?"

"Not even remotely. But I wouldn't mind knowing if Cassidy Yorke's going to be around for a while, or if she's just passing through my life."

Even though she knew better, Cassidy found it very easy to convince herself that he really cared whether or not she stayed. "Actually, I haven't made up my mind yet. It sounds great—terrific pay, lots of perks, good exposure."

"But?" he urged, responding to the doubt in her voice.

"And if the same thing happens out there? Do I just pack up and move again? When do I stand my ground and fight for what I want?" She sighed, staring at the ceiling. "I could be damned good if they'd give me a chance, that's what's so frustrating! News anchor could be the beginning of something, but it could just as easily be another dead end. I don't want to simply *read* the news, I want to report it. And I don't want to be just another pretty face on the six o'clock news!" It took her a long moment to realize that Logan was staring down at her, a half smile playing around his mouth.

She blushed. "There I go again! You must think I'm incredibly arrogant."

"Arrogant?" He laughed, shaking his head. "No, not arrogant. Just confident. There's a lot of difference."

Cassidy smiled ruefully. "A couple of people at KALB might argue that point. I'm starting to get a reputation for being difficult."

"Seems to me," Logan said quietly, "that a label like that is only relative, considering that you're co-hosting with one of the biggest egos in television."

"Except Marsh Wheeler's been in the business long enough to have earned the right. I haven't. Even in an occupation filled with big egos, being labeled 'difficult' this early in my career can sink me. The competition is deadly!"

"So you're wondering if you should go along with what they want and not make waves."

He said it bluntly, but without accusation or judgment. Cassidy looked at him. "The thought's crossed my mind," she admitted quietly. "I love this business, Logan, but I'm not stupid. Or naive. I'm good, but there are a hundred other Cassidy Yorkes out there just as good—Cassidy Yorkes who would give the station what they want without a whimper of complaint. Sometimes I wonder if I'd be smarter to swallow my pride and go along with the ratings until I've earned my stripes, and the weight that goes with them."

"You don't believe that."

He said it so matter-of-factly that Cassidy stared at him. Then she laughed. "How do you know so much about me, anyway?"

Logan smiled. "Because we're a lot alike, Cassidy Yorke." He still had one arm resting along the edge of the tub behind her and he cupped her shoulder with his hand, caressing her damp skin almost absently. Suddenly pensive and thoughtful, he frowned. "Don't sell out, Cass. Integrity's something you never think about until it's too late.

And every time you sell out, you sell a bit more of yourself."

Cassidy looked at him curiously. He was sitting so close to her that his chest pressed against her shoulder and arm. He'd draped his other arm over her wet, upraised knee, one long leg braced against the far side of the tub, the other tucked up so his thigh rested snugly against her bottom. Without really thinking about it, she reached up and touched his cheek, leaving a trail of sparkling water drops on the tanned skin.

His eyes caught hers and for a split moment she thought he was going to say something else. Then the mood vanished. He turned his head and kissed her hand, delicately licking the warm water from her fingers. She ran her thumb lightly across his mouth and he closed his lips around it, sucking on it gently. He released it after a moment and moved nearer to her. His breath tickled her mouth and Cassidy swallowed. She ran her fingers across his shoulder and let them rest lightly on the back of his neck, moving her cheek against the satiny smoothness of his. His mouth moved on her throat and ear in lingering, warm little kisses that made her go weak.

"Oh, Logan," she breathed. "If I had any sense at all, I'd go home before..." She let it trail off, closing her eyes as he nuzzled her ear.

"Before?" he murmured, running his mouth along the angle of her jaw. "Before what, Cass?"

"You know," she breathed.

"Do you want to go home?"

It needed no saying, she knew that already. Just as he must have known merely by reading it there in her eyes. She hadn't even been aware of making the decision, yet it had been made. Seconds ago, perhaps even hours—it didn't really matter. All that mattered was that she was certain it was the right answer—not just the one that he wanted to hear, but right for her too.

"No," she whispered, hearing her voice as though it belonged to a stranger. "No, Logan, I don't want to go home."

"What *do* you want, Cass?"

"I want to stay with you tonight," she breathed, drawing his mouth down to hers. "I want you to make love to me."

Four

Logan smiled. "I was hoping you'd say that," he murmured. He cupped her throat in his wet hand and bent down to her mouth.

He kissed her with consummate skill, his tongue slipping deeply into her mouth. A syrupy heat spilled through her and settled taut and urgent in her lower stomach. Cassidy gave a little sigh of pleasure as his tongue moved coaxingly against hers in an explicit rhythm that sent electric shivers through her. She clutched at him, tangling her legs with his to anchor herself against the force of the swirling water. Logan gave a throaty growl of pleasure and pulled her urgently against him. Cassidy had to struggle to catch her breath as he moved his hips against her.

Very gently, he slid his fingers under the elastic along the top of the bodysuit and eased it down over one breast. It gleamed whitely in the water, pearl-like against her own tan and Logan's sunbrowned hand. Arching her back, Cassidy lifted both breasts clear of the water, sinking her fingers into the thick, damp curls on the back of Logan's neck as he settled his mouth over the wet nipple. She gave a tiny gasp as his tongue caressed the hardening bud, and she felt his body respond to her growing arousal.

Using both hands, he drew the suit down to her hips. The jets of bubbling water were incredibly erotic against her bare skin and she stretched sinuously, loving the feel of both the water and Logan's hands on her. He let go of her suddenly and she gave a gasp as she started to slip under water.

"Sorry," he apologized with a breathless laugh. "Hang on for a second." He twisted away from her, thrashing around in the already foaming water.

Laughing as she tried to keep her head above water, Cassidy wrapped her arms around Logan's neck. "What are you—oh!" She sucked in a startled breath as he pulled her firmly against him, his now naked body so explicitly, aggressively male that it literally took her breath away. Instinctively, she shifted to accommodate him, taking him fully between her thighs. Logan groaned softly. He moved against her and Cassidy gasped, thighs tightening, as his urgent thrusts triggered a spasm of the most incredible sensations she'd ever experienced.

She stiffened. "Log—Logan!" Unbelievably, that swelling, building wave crested, broke, spilled through her, hot as lava. She shuddered uncontrollably, groaning softly as she went limp in Logan's arms.

Dazed, she murmured something that was half protest and half encouragement as Logan drew his fingers lightly up her inner thigh. He touched her lightly through the thin fabric of the bodysuit and she went motionless, still so sensitive that even that feather-touch threatened to send her over the edge again. She caught his wrist, torn between pushing him away and pressing his hand more firmly against her.

"Show me what you want," Logan whispered, the raw desire in his voice sending another wave of weakness through Cassidy. "Like this? Or this . . . ?"

Cassidy arched against him, eyes closed. "Oh, Logan!"

He gave a grunt of delighted surprise as his caressing fingers found her bodysuit fasteners. He flicked them free and the bodysuit parted smoothly. She moaned softly as the flimsy barricade vanished between her and his gently searching hand. He let them roll gently with the force of the water until they were lying side by side, one arm under her shoulders to keep her head above water. He kissed her with a deep, unhurried thoroughness and Cassidy relaxed against him, loosening the muscles in her thighs that had tightened instinctively at his first probing touch.

"You're so warm and soft," Logan whispered against her mouth. "Like velvet, waiting for me."

Cassidy lifted her hips against the gently intrusive touch. It seemed impossible that he could repeat that first unexpected magic, that she would experience that same exquisite, breathtaking pleasure again. But she did. It was even better this time, the peak higher and more powerful than before, the downsliding ebb lasting longer, carrying her further.

Logan held her tightly as the pulsing tremors slowly abated. "You're so beautiful," he whispered. "I can feel you take flame. It's like holding the heart of a volcano in my hand."

But Cassidy only half heard him. What on earth was happening to her, she wondered dazedly. This was a part of her that she had never suspected existed, yet Logan had found and kindled all those unexplored passions so easily. Or had she always suspected they were there, simply awaiting the right man, the right time? Is that what had drawn her to Logan tonight—some ancient female instinct for what was right for her, for what she needed?

She opened her eyes, finding Logan watching her intently. "Touch me," he whispered grittily. "You don't have to be shy with me, Cass. Not now."

She put her hand out hesitantly. Logan closed his eyes with a groan as, delicate and shy in her inexperience, she touched him, marveling at his perfection, the controlled strength, the vital response even that tentative gesture elicited. He looked down at her, eyes smoldering with his need, as she caressed him, the instinctive desire to please him making up for her inexperience. "Maybe we should get out of here," he murmured a moment later. "I don't think anyone's ever drowned making love in a whirlpool, but it's taking more concentration than I've got just now to keep my head above water. And I'd rather be concentrating on you. But first, let's get rid of this." He tugged the bodysuit over her hips.

Cassidy kicked her legs free and, naked, she slipped her arms around his neck and pressed herself against him. "Much better!"

"My God, Cass!" he protested with a gasping laugh. "I'm trying my best to hang on to what little self-control I've got left."

"I can't imagine why," Cassidy teased, pleasantly shocked by the passionate hunger this man aroused in her. Shocked, too, by her uninhibited responses to that hunger as she moved against him eagerly, delighting in the unfamiliar male angles and contours of him. "I seem to have the most interesting effect on you. What happens to your willpower when I do this? Or this . . . ?"

"Cassidy!" Laughing, he snatched her hand away and stood, pulling her up with him. "I'll show you exactly what kind of an effect you're having on me!" He caught her against him and stepped out of the tub, striding toward the huge bed with her.

Naked and wet, they fell back on the bed together, legs and arms tangled, mouths locked in a dizzying kiss. The fur bedspread felt sensuously decadent under her and Cassidy laughingly tore her mouth from Logan's urgent kiss. "Logan wait! We're going to ruin the fur!"

"Then let me dry you," he growled, licking her breasts, then running his tongue down across her stomach in a lazy spiral. "You taste delicious."

"Logan!" Cassidy's eyes widened with delighted shock as his mouth wandered downward, flicking tongue lapping at the water glistening on her skin. He eased her thighs apart with gentle persistence and delicately nuzzled the secret, hidden warmth of her. Cassidy moaned his name and lifted her hips, as shocked by her eager acceptance of this intimacy as she was by the rest of this totally unexpected evening.

"I hope you weren't expecting whipped cream and acrobatics tonight," Logan whispered, suddenly beside her again, his mouth hot and damply sweet on hers. He cupped her head in both palms, raining biting little kisses over her face as he eased his long legs between hers. "Because quite honestly, Cass, I can't wait any longer. I want to make love to you now—no games, no complicated maneuvers. I just want you, all of you, now."

"Yes!" gasped Cassidy, catching her breath as he moved his hips sharply to bring them together in that final and most intimate joining. She arched upward with a shuddering moan, eyes closed, head thrown back, straining against him to make that first claim as total and deeply complete as physically possible.

Logan groaned her name, his mouth settling over hers in a hot, drugging kiss that sent the last of Cassidy's inhibitions scattering. Arms locked around his waist, she moved wantonly under him, driven half-wild by his whispers of encouragement, whispering things in return that she'd never imagined saying. Logan made love masterfully and hard, his lean body driving into hers with exactly the aggressive fierceness she craved. It was as though he wanted to leave no doubt about his claim to her, as though he could somehow imprint part of his own being onto hers.

And again her body responded vitally to him, transporting her to the highest reaches of an ecstasy she'd only imagined possible. It ebbed slowly, tingling through her in waves of lessening intensity until she could breathe again. Only this time she wasn't alone. Logan straightened his arms, rearing over her, head thrown back as he shouted her name in triumph and satisfaction. Then he gave a final convulsive shudder and let his head fall forward until his hair brushed her face. Cassidy reached up and cradled his sweat-damp face in her hands and after a moment he lowered himself over her again, panting, his heart racing against hers.

"My God!" he whispered hoarsely. "You ought to come with a warning label—contents explosive, handle with care!" He cradled her against him. "I'm supposed to be the expert at all this, but tonight you've shown me I haven't even scratched the surface." He kissed the corner of her mouth. "You've given an entire new meaning to the phrase 'making love.'"

"Material for a new book," she teased, kissing his chin.

Logan stiffened slightly. "No. I don't think so."

"No?" Cassidy gave a mischievous laugh. "Darn, and here I thought I'd rate a whole chapter, at least!"

Logan stared down at her. His eyes seemed suddenly cool. Saying nothing, he rolled onto his back, not touching her. "Is that what you thought tonight was?" he asked in a clipped, remote voice, staring at the ceiling. "Research?"

His anger took Cassidy by surprise. She rolled onto her side to look at him, bewildered at his abrupt mood change. "Not entirely," she said lightly, trying to tease him back into good humor. "But I thought writers always wound up running their experiences through the old typewriter at some time or another."

"Not this writer." A muscle pulsed in his cheek. Still, he didn't look at her, staring angrily at the shadowed ceiling.

Cassidy lay there uncertainly for a moment, then reached out and put her hand on his arm tentatively. "Logan, I didn't mean that the way it sounded. Of course I don't think you made love to me tonight just as part of a research project. Do you think I'd be here if I believed that?"

He turned his head. Then, suddenly, he smiled, his anger vanishing as abruptly as it had erupted. "No," he murmured, reaching up and running the back of his hand down her cheek. "Sorry for snapping at you like that. Just call it reflex action. It's just that Logan Wilde's motives are always suspect when a woman's involved. I guess I'm a little defensive."

Cassidy gave a quiet laugh, snuggling comfortably against the damp warmth of him. "You talk about Logan Wilde as though he were someone else. What devious secret have I uncovered, anyway?"

Logan gave her a startled look and she thought for an instant that he was going to say something. Then he simply smiled mysteriously and cupped her face in his palm, kissing her lightly. "Don't go away." He turned and swung his legs over the side of the bed. "I vaguely remember promising you an espresso before I was swept off my feet and thoroughly seduced."

"Who seduced who?" Cassidy protested sleepily.

"Whom," Logan corrected with a lazy smile. "And I think it was a mutual affair. Which," he added, drawing his fingertips lightly down her hip, "is the only way seduction should be done."

"I'm beginning to think that there may be parts of Logan Wilde's philosophy that even a country kid from Oregon might find enlightening."

"I'd be delighted to participate in any research you'd like to conduct on the matter," Logan drawled. "After all, I have a fairly intimate knowledge of the man's works."

"I'd love to become more intimately acquainted with the man's works myself," Cassidy murmured with a wicked chuckle, her hand straying playfully. "His books, too."

"You've got a delectably lewd mind," Logan said with an appreciative grin. "I foresee spending many long, pleasant hours becoming intimately acquainted with each other, Miss Yorke. In fact, I suspect we'll become intimately acquainted at least a couple of times more before morning."

An anticipatory shiver ran through Cassidy as Logan's eyes met hers, warm with promise. Then he stood up and she watched the play of muscles in his thighs and lean buttocks as he walked away from her.

Cassidy pushed the fur spread down and slipped between the royal-blue satin sheets. It was like sliding naked into cool water, the feel of the satin against her love-warmed skin so sensuously erotic that she smiled to herself. What else would Logan Wilde have on his bed? She reached for her evening bag on the low dresser and took out a tiny vial of perfume. Smile widening, she touched the glass stopper to her throat, behind her ears, between her breasts. *Vanity, thy name is woman*, she chided herself with amusement tucking the bottle back into her bag hastily when she heard Logan's jaunty whistling. He appeared at the bedroom door just as she snapped her bag closed, and she stuffed it in a pile of pillows, mildy embarrassed at being caught primping.

"Espresso, as promised." Logan set the tray down and reached across her to arrange the pillows into a back rest. Her evening bag tumbled across the slippery sheets and he caught it with a laugh, tossing it aside. "You women and your purses! I think you'd all rather be caught stark naked than without your—"

He stopped so abruptly that Cassidy, her mouth already half-open for a laughing rebuttal, looked up at him. He was staring at something intently, his eyes showing a stunned disbelief that changed, even as she watched, to icy rage.

"Logan?" Cassidy sat up. "What on earth is the matter?" She followed his gaze to where her evening bag lay. It had come open, spilling lipstick and eyeshadow pencils across the fur spread. But they weren't what Logan was staring at. It was the other thing that lay among them, small and black and glittering.

"Oh, damn!" Cassidy reached guiltily for the tiny tape recorder. "Logan, I can explain this."

His hand shot out and caught her wrist, his fingers tightening so fiercely that Cassidy gasped. "I'll just bet you can," he said in a voice as cold and cutting as an Arctic wind. "I'll bet you have an answer to this like you've had an answer to everything tonight."

"Logan!" Cassidy tried to twist her arm free. "Logan, this isn't what it looks like!"

"No?" he asked silkily, his fingers tightening with brutal ferocity. "And just what the hell is it supposed to look like, Cassidy?" He picked up the recorder and thrust it toward her, his lips twisting with fury. "Did you get it all, Cass? Did you get every word and groan and whisper? Are you going to go back and dub in a running commentary so your listeners know exactly what was happening?"

"Logan!" It shocked her so badly that Cassidy simply stared at him, mouth open, eyes wide with disbelief. "My God! You don't think that I . . ." It was too insane, too horrible, to even say aloud.

"Come on, Cassidy," he suggested with deceptive good-humor. "You can stop playing the role now, okay? You're a bright, ambitious kind of woman, you told me so yourself. And a detailed, blow-by-blow account of the famous Logan Wilde in action would really send your ratings sky-high."

Cassidy shook her head in bewildered denial. "You can't possibly believe that I was actually recording while we made love," she whispered raggedly, feeling absolutely sick. "My God, Logan, what kind of woman do you think I am?"

"The kind of woman who's damned good at what she does—your exact words, remember?" He gave her wrist a twist that made her bite her lip to keep from crying out. "The kind of woman who knows exactly where she wants to be in five years, and who's willing to do whatever's necessary to get there."

Suddenly he flung her from him and lunged to his feet, tossing the tape recorder across the room. He glared down at her, his face so angry that Cassidy flinched as though he'd struck her. "Well? Was I everything you expected? Did the great lover live up to his *reputation*?" He spat the word as he might an obscenity. "I sure as hell hope so. A man can't be too careful when dealing with the media, after all. One critical word from you on-air tomorrow night, and my *reputation* could be finished!"

Cassidy's cheeks flared, the sharp sting of anger rousing her from stunned silence. "Is that what you think?" she asked disbelievingly. "That I slept with you to see if you lived up to your billing?"

"You wouldn't be the first," he assured her in a mocking drawl.

It was a vicious gibe, calculated to hurt. And it did. Cheeks burning, Cassidy gave her head a toss. "Well, you don't have to worry," she assured him furiously, "because you were everything I expected! You're a fantastic lover, Logan—everything a woman could possibly want in bed. If you want to use me as a recommendation, feel free!"

This time Logan flushed, his azure eyes almost black with anger. "Thanks, but I have more than I can handle now," he said with deliberate crudity. "But if you want me to return the favor, don't hesitate to give me a call. You're not half-bad yourself."

Cassidy recoiled, eyes stinging with sudden tears, too hurt and angry to even defend herself against Logan's vicious accusations.

He stared down at her, his eyes bleak. "God, what a damned fool I was," he whispered hoarsely. "I'd actually convinced myself that you were different, that tonight was—" He caught himself. His lip curled. "But I had you pegged right all along, didn't I? Although I'll admit one thing. You had me fooled there at the end. I figured you for an amateur. I really didn't think you'd go the limit."

"But it didn't stop you, did it?" Cassidy shot back in outrage. "You made love with me tonight in spite of believing that I was simply researching your 'technique!' If that makes me an opportunist, what does it make you?"

Logan's eyes narrowed dangerously. "As gullible as hell, for one thing."

"Oh, don't play the self-righteous victim with me. The only reason you even asked me out tonight was because I presented a challenge to that fatuous ego of yours! Because you wanted to prove that you could seduce any woman you wanted—including me!" Nostrils flared, Cassidy rocked up onto her knees. "What happened to all that high-flying moralizing about *making love* versus using someone for your own pleasure, tell me that? We were both used!" Cassidy stopped to catch her breath, shaking with anger and hurt.

Logan flushed darkly. "I think you'd better leave," he said in a rough voice, turning away. "I don't perform on demand. And I'm not interested in providing you with any more material for your show. I suspect you have enough to keep New Mexico entertained for an hour or two at least."

His curt dismissal was the last straw. Tears of shame and hurt welled in Cassidy's eyes. Refusing to show him this final victory, she slid out of bed and stumbled blindly toward the low leather chair where her dress lay. Something glittered in the carpet at her feet and she stared at it for a moment, then knelt down and picked up the tape recorder.

Hugging her dress against her, she glanced around at Logan. "You were right about tonight," she whispered. "I did go out with you planning on getting a story for tomorrow night's show. I brought the recorder hoping to get a few classic Wilde lines down for posterity. But then something... changed. Between you and me. I—" She caught herself, realizing that he'd probably heard the same story a hundred times from a hundred adoring women. She tossed the tape recorder onto the bed between them. "If you'd taken the time to listen to this, you'd know that I turned it off somewhere between the Grand Marnier and the second kiss."

Logan was staring warily at her, as though waiting for some trick, some final admission that it had all been a game. Her gaze faltered and she looked away. "There won't be a follow-up show on Logan Wilde," she whispered. "Tomorrow night, or any other night." Then, still clutching the crumpled dress protectively against her, she turned and half-ran toward the nearest door, slamming it behind her.

Shivering uncontrollably, Cassidy took several deep, unsteady breaths, blinking rapidly to clear her eyes as she pulled the dress on. Two tears escaped and trickled down her cheeks, and she dabbed at them with the back of her hand, furious at herself for allowing him to hurt her like this. Something moved across the room from her and she stared at the pale, wide-eyed woman there for a full minute before she realized she was looking at her own reflection. She gave a strangled laugh and closed her eyes in relief. She had thought for half an instant that she'd encountered a forgotten remnant of another of Logan Wilde's tempestuous nights!

Feeling calmer, she looked around her. She was in a small dressing room complete with every accoutrement for the perfect bachelor. Idly, she pulled open a shallow drawer in the built-in vanity, somehow not surprised to discover a collection of women's cosmetics that would put most department stores to shame. She picked up a bottle or two, smiling. Wilde was, if nothing else, eclectic in his taste in women. Blonde, brunette, redhead. There probably wasn't a woman in the world who wouldn't be able to find what she needed here to repair the ravages of a dip in the hot tub and a night of lovemaking. Cassidy swallowed a mad desire to laugh. Did the man leave nothing to chance?

It seemed a shame to waste them. She quickly wiped off her make-up and brushed her hair out, finally daring to meet her eyes in the mirror. How ironic, being accused of using casual sex to get what she wanted by the master of casual sex himself. She sighed, putting the brush down. Perhaps tomorrow she would be able to see the humor in it; right now she just wanted to escape this nightmare, and go home.

Logan was sitting on the edge of the bed when she came out. He had pulled on a pair of pale blue briefs and was staring down at the white sweater in his hands. He glanced up at her, his eyes shadowed and unreadable. The anger seemed burned out of him and Cassidy's own outrage dissipated. She wanted to say something, to take back the cruel words and accusations, but then she realized that nothing she could say now mattered. The magic between them had been destroyed. It didn't matter any more what he believed. She wiped a stray tear from her cheek with the back of her hand and silently walked from the room.

The concierge answered the phone on the first ring. He sounded startled when she asked him to call a cab for her, as though he wasn't used to having Logan's women reappear before dawn. She smiled slightly, repeating her request. There's a first time for everything, she advised him silently; even the great Logan Wilde loses one now and again.

A hand came from behind her and Logan took the receiver from her and spoke into it. "Don't bother, Walter," he said quietly. "We'll use my car."

"I can take a cab," Cassidy insisted, not looking at him.

"I brought you here; I'll take you home."

"Gallant to the end." She walked stiffly toward the door and pulled it open, waiting by the elevator for Logan. He joined her in a moment, carrying a cream colored overcoat which he draped around her shoulders before she could protest.

"If you're as naked under that dress as I think you are," he said gruffly, "you'll catch pneumonia out there tonight."

"Thank you," Cassidy whispered. There didn't seem to be anything else left to say, so she simply followed him into the elevator.

Apart from asking her address, Logan said nothing during the drive to her apartment. Cassidy stayed just as silent, huddled miserably in the bucket seat clutching Logan's coat around her. She glanced at him now and again, but he seemed oblivious to her, staring out at the sparse traffic in thoughtful preoccupation. He pulled up at the entrance of her apartment building and shut the engine off. The silence was loud, and Cassidy could hear the Ferrari's hood pop as it cooled. "Thanks for the coat," she whispered, shrugging out of its warmth and draping it over the seat back. "Good night."

"Wait."

His voice was rough. Cassidy paused, hand on the door handle, and glanced around at him. He was staring out the windshield, one arm draped over the steering wheel. Suddenly he breathed a weary oath and ran his fingers through his hair, turning in the seat to look at her. "Look, Cass, I've made just about every stupid mistake tonight that it's possible for a man to make. I want to apologize, but I don't even know where to begin." He rubbed his eyes wearily. "God, what a mess! Logan Wilde, the guy who's supposed to have all the answers."

Cassidy found herself smiling. "We could shake hands, go to our own corners and pretend none of it ever happened."

He gave her a sharp glance, as though suspecting she was laughing at him. Then his own mouth curved in a faint smile. "Don't make it easy for me. I acted like an idiot back there."

"We both acted like idiots," she corrected. "I had no business playing investigative reporter with that tape recorder in the first place."

He gave a quiet laugh, shaking his head. His gaze brushed her features one at a time, lingering on her mouth for a wistful moment before meeting her eyes again. "You're a very special woman, Cass Yorke."

"Does this mean we're not fighting anymore?"

He gave another snort of laughter, some of the lines and weariness leaving his face. "Yeah, Miss Yorke, I think this means we're not fighting anymore." He leaned across and opened her door. "Come on. The sooner I get you home, the less chance I have of making a bigger fool of myself than I have already."

Together, they walked up to her apartment. He took the key from her hand and unlocked the door, then reached in and turned the hall light on for her. "No roommate waiting up?"

"No roommate." She smiled, wondering if it was a subtle hint that he'd like to be asked in.

But while she was contemplating doing just that, he bent down and kissed her gently on the mouth. She stepped nearer instinctively and his mouth lingered, then settled on hers more firmly. They kissed with the leisurely familiarity of old lovers, Logan's mouth moving on hers with a controlled hunger that echoed their earlier passion.

He drew his mouth from hers slowly, running his lips across her cheek. "I wish I'd met you about a hundred years ago," he murmured. "Back before we got all tangled up in roles and games." Then, as though catching himself, he drew back and started to turn away. "Good night, Cass." He smiled, then walked briskly down the corridor to the elevators. Cassidy ached to call him back. But she swallowed the temptation and stepped inside her apartment instead, closing the door firmly and locking it before she could change her mind.

There was a thump from the bedroom and an instant later a calico cat appeared, tail aloft. It wound itself around her ankles, purring loudly, and Cassidy picked it up and buried her face in the thick fur. "Oh, Sam, what am I going to do? I think I fell in love tonight."

Sam meowed sympathetically and rubbed her head under Cassidy's chin. "You gave up all that nonsense years ago, didn't you, old girl?" Sam acknowledged the accusation by purring even louder and Cassidy gave her a hug. "Did Mrs. Gillespie come in and feed you?" She checked the cat's food and water dishes, glad to see that the woman who lived in the next apartment had indeed been in. "She spoils you worse than I do," Cassidy muttered to the cat, eyeing her good soup bowl which was now half-filled with dry kibble. "It's late, cat. Let's go to bed, and I'll tell you all about Logan Wilde."

Five

Cassidy knew that she was going to be the subject of a few curious questions about her date with Wilde the next morning, but she didn't realize that the entire station was going to pounce on her. She'd scarcely closed the door behind her when people started crowding around, avid for every detail. She fielded all the questions easily, managing to convince everyone that she was telling them a great deal while in fact admitting very little. But gradually, as curiosities waned, the day settled back to normal.

Her twelve o'clock news spot over, she settled into preparing for that evening's edition of *Headliners*, an interview with two Alamogordo men who claimed to have been kidnapped by aliens from space. She and a film crew had spent an entire day interviewing the two, taking shots of the landing site, photographing patches of scorched grass and some peculiar marks in the sand near the spot where the two claimed to have been whisked up into the spaceship on a beam of blue light. It was all an obvious fabrication, and not a particularly good one at that. Their story was a word-for-word retelling of a similiar incident that had supposedly taken place in Texas a month earlier, and the spaceship itself was a faithful duplicate of Captain Kirk's trusty *Enterprise*. There was the usual blurred photograph that could have been anything from a flying saucer to a soaring eagle. And the usual "souvenir," a piece of metal that one of them had managed to slip into his pocket before being released, and that the camera operator had identified as a piston ring from a '63 Chevy pickup.

Ordinarily, she would have handled the story good-naturedly, not actually giving it credence, but not actually ridiculing it either. But today she found herself editing the tape viciously, showing the two as a pair of not too bright, publicity hungry frauds. Her own impatience shocked her. Finally she simply gave up and turned the entire thing over to the editing assistant, breaking her own rule about editing her own tapes and lifting a few eyebrows over this bizarre departure from her usual meticulous professionalism.

To hell with the rumors, she decided irritably, ignoring the speculative looks following her as she stalked out of the editing room. She stopped to get herself a cup of black coffee, then retreated to the relative privacy of the dressing room. To her relief, Marsh wasn't there. She sank into his armchair with a sigh, wishing her head would stop pounding.

It was all Logan Wilde's fault! She had gotten about an hour's sleep last night, spending most of the night tossing and turning, able to think of nothing but the exquisite wonder of his lovemaking and then the anger and bitterness that followed. Although, she had to revise grudgingly, if she had been a little more circumspect about resisting that Logan Wilde charm in the first place, none of it would have happened. So who was more to blame: Wilde for simply being the man he was, or her for becoming—for a short wonderous while—someone she wasn't?

She frowned as she rubbed her throbbing temples. This brooding was senseless. It had happened, that's all; setting blame and looking for profound answers was a waste of time.

"Ah, here she is! The lady herself!"

The voice intruded harshly into Cassidy's reverie. She looked up and smiled thinly at Marsh, trying to cast off her moodiness. She started to get up but he waved her to stay where she was and settled into the other chair with uncharacteristic expansiveness.

"Well, darling, how's it going? You look a little peaked, if you don't mind my saying so. Long night?"

Cassidy gave him a sharp look.

Marsh's eyes widened with innocence. "I was simply wondering if you had an enjoyable evening with Mr. Wilde."

"Not particularly."

Marsh leaned forward, smiling lasciviously. "Come on now, Cass darling—you can tell me. Did you . . . ?"

"Honestly, Marsh! You, too?"

Marsh shrugged expressively. "Well, darling, the question's an obvious one! I mean, after all, you're an attractive woman and our Mr. Wilde is not without a certain physical appeal. The situation lends itself to speculation, you'll have to admit. One could not blame you for indulging in a bit of—"

"Marsh!" Cassidy's voice rose warningly. "I don't know why my private life's suddenly become such a topic for conversation around here, but I don't want to hear another word about Logan Wilde!"

"Of course, darling."

"And quit looking at me like that! Last night was just a date. We had dinner, we talked, he drove me home."

"And that's all."

"Yes, that's all," she lied boldly.

"In other words, no story."

"Exactly."

"Small wonder Vaughn's gnashing his teeth," Marsh drawled companionably. "Our Mr. Vaughn has his eyes set on bigger things, you know. I think he had his heart set on a hot exposé of Logan Wilde's love secrets."

"Well, it's too bad about Ken Vaughn," Cassidy muttered. "If he'd listened to me in the first place, we wouldn't be wasting our time with stories like this anyway."

There was a brisk tap at the door. It opened and Jeri Martell popped her head in. "Oh, good. You're here." She came in and sat on the end of the cluttered dressing table, the inevitable clipboard with its thick wad of paper clutched across her chest. "How would you like to anchor the coverage for the city council elections the week after next?"

"Oh, God, I hate those things!" Marsh complained. "They go on forever, and you're stuck on-camera half the night trying to pretend you really care who wins. Small town politics are *such* a bore."

"Then you'll be glad to know that I wasn't talking to you," Jeri said very pleasantly. "The boys upstairs want Cass, not you."

Marsh seemed to stiffen slightly. He looked at Jeri, his face curiously devoid of any expression. "Cassidy?"

"Cassidy," Jeri replied, still pleasant. "You'd better watch out, Marsh. If Cass gets much more popular around here, you could be out of a job."

"Somehow I doubt that," Cassidy put in smoothly, feeling a sudden coolness in the room. "I suspect it's more likely that they're sending me to cover the elections to free Marsh for something more important."

"Yeah," Jeri drawled with a laugh. "Like the Celebrity Jamboree the local hot air balloon clubs are putting on this weekend."

"Hot air balloons?" Marsh asked in disbelief.

"Yep. Saturday. They're drumming up money and support for the Colonel Cecil Hutcheson Chronic Care Facility. All the local TV and radio stations have teams entered. Tex McGuire and Jackson dePaul from the news department are flying KALB's entry. And Crothers wants lots of support for them."

"My God, what next!" Marsh fumed. "Last month it was a 'Save the Petroglyphs' campaign, and then that 'Pennies for Puppies' thing for the Humane people. And what was that excruciatingly tasteless business with the wheelchairs . . . ?"

"The Wheelchair Rodeo for physically disabled kids over at St. Joseph's," Jeri reminded him with a slight edge to her voice. "All of which Cassidy handled."

"Precisely," he snapped. "I do not make celebrity appearances."

"You are this time," Jeri advised him calmly. "You're scheduled to be there at six-thirty. Sharp. That's A.M., Marsh."

"We'll see about that!"

Jeri shrugged indifferently. "You'd better get used to it, Marsh. All the promo requests we're getting lately are for Cassidy. You seem to be old news."

Marsh's eyes glittered balefully. "If I were you," he advised her sweetly, "I'd remember that jobs in the television industry are hard to come by these days. Especially should one get a reputation for being . . . difficult."

This time Cassidy stiffened. Jeri simply laughed. "You should know, Marsh," she taunted.

Cassidy held her breath. Marsh's face mottled and he stood up abruptly, eyes filled with malevolence. "One of these days, my girl, you're going to go one step too far." He turned on one heel and strode from the room, pulling the door closed behind him with a bang.

Cassidy eased her breath out. "You really enjoy living dangerously, don't you?"

"Pompous jackass," Jeri said calmly. "No wonder they want him to cover the balloon rally. He even looks like one. Big, round and full of hot air."

Cassidy smiled tolerantly, familiar with Jeri's antagonism toward Marsh. "Your timing was dead-on, as usual—

an hour before we go on-air. I feel sorry for the poor victim he's interviewing today. Who is it, anyway?''

Jeri looked down at her clipboard. ''The director of that new women's shelter on Tijeras Avenue.''

''Janis Chavez?'' Cassidy sat up, astounded. ''Damn it, that was my story! How did Marsh get it?''

Jeri raised an eyebrow. ''How does Marsh get anything around here? He decided he wanted it, then bullied the fifth floor into giving it to him.'' She gave a malicious smile. ''One of these days the boys up on the fifth are going to realize what every major TV station in the country knows: that Marsh Wheeler isn't half as good as he thinks he is. And I hope I'm around when he makes his weekly threat to quit, and someone finally takes him up on it.''

''Frankly,'' Cassidy said in exasperation, ''I agree with you at the moment. The Bright Angel Center isn't Marsh's kind of story. They need a sympathetic angle to get all the public support they can. You know how Marsh feels about social programs of any kind, but especially programs aimed at women. He'll confront Chavez about 'wasting taxpayers' money,' antagonize her and three-quarters of the women watching the show and make the whole thing sound like an expensive joke. Honestly, what was Ken Vaughn thinking about?''

''Ratings,'' drawled Jeri. ''He doesn't care that the Bright Angel is desperately needed, or that we can help—or hinder—its funding. He just knows that a Marsh Wheeler interview will stir up a lot of public opinion. That means viewers. And that, dear Cassidy, is the name of the game.'' She slid off the dressing table and started toward the door. ''Is it a go for the election?''

''Yes, I'll cover their damned election!'' Cassidy replied heatedly. ''God knows, I can't get into much trouble playing my 'bright, vivacious TV anchor' role, can I? What's Marsh doing that weekend? Interviewing the president?''

Jeri smiled sympathetically. ''Not that I know of, but don't put it past him.'' She pulled the door open, looking around. "He's starting to feel you gaining, Cass. And Marsh Wheeler's not a good loser. A lot of us here at KALB are behind you all the way, but if Wheeler decides you're a real threat..." She left it hanging, her expression serious. "Just watch out for him, all right?"

Cassidy laughed quietly. "Aren't you being a bit dramatic?"

"He's antagonized every TV exec from New York to Los Angeles, Cassidy. Do you really think he'd have taken a job with a little backwater station like KALB unless it was all he could get? He was on top of the heap once, the *enfant terrible* of the television talk shows. Every station in North America was fighting to get him and he was demanding—and getting—the top money in the business. Then he started to believe his own hype. But people got tired of his constant put-downs, his sarcasm, his tastelessness, and Mr. Talk Show himself suddenly found himself out of work. He's a faded rose now, Cass. He's bitter—and he's scared. So keep your eye on him."

"All right," Cassidy assured her with an indulgent smile. "I will. Thanks for the warning. And the concern."

Jeri grinned and gave her a thumbs-up sign as she left.

Cassidy sat for a long, thoughtful while after Jeri had left, mug of cold coffee cupped forgotten in her hands. She didn't know who she was angrier with: Ken for giving Marsh her Chavez interview, or Marsh for taking it.

Someone knocked on the door gently. "Who is it?" Cassidy snapped, sitting up and slamming her mug down.

"Just me, Miss Yorke." Andy Neiman, the new editorial assistant, peeked tentatively around the door.

"What is it?" He flinched visibly at her tone, and Cassidy sighed inwardly. "Sorry, Andy," she said more quietly. "Come on in."

He responded to the invitation like a spaniel pup to a gentle word, grinning from ear to ear with embarrassed delight as he edged into the room. As always, Cassidy felt sorry for him. Tall and gangling and always trying too hard, he was about as low on the station hierarchy as it was possible to get. She remembered all too well her own days as station *gofer* in Oregon when she was just starting out, and always tried to make his life a little easier. She looked at him expectantly.

"Oh! Yeah!" He blushed, fumbling with a wad of crumpled paper. "Video's finished with your UFO tape and wants you to look at it. And Mr. Craig needs to know if you want the tape run at the beginning of your spot with a voice-over, at the end, or somewhere in the middle. You—uh—" Andy shuffled his feet, looking spectacularly uncomfortable. "You didn't, well, give him a script or anything."

"Oh, darn, I forgot," Cassidy breathed, irritated at her own carelessness. "Thanks, Andy. Tell video I'll be right there, and tell Dick I'll go over the show format with him as soon as I okay the tape. And, hey—" Already half out the door, Andy looked around at her nervously. Cassidy smiled at him. "I didn't mean to take your head off like that. You caught me on a bad day. Sorry."

"Oh, gee, that's okay, Miss Yorke." He beamed at her. "I know you didn't mean it. You're one of the nicest people at KALB." Blushing furiously, he gave her one last stricken look and fled.

Cassidy grinned, feeling some of her anger and impatience dissipate. No matter what nonsense she had to put up with from Ken and the fifth floor, at least she had one adoring fan. She took a deep breath, already feeling better, and smiled at her reflection as she walked to the door. "Get to work, Yorke," she advised herself dryly. "There's no room at this station for more than one oversized ego, and Marsh already has that role all tied up!"

To Cassidy's surprise, her show that evening went very well. Video had done a terrific job editing her tape, and Dick did his usual director's magic. He pulled the show together into a smooth, professional production that brought her more than the usual number of congratulatory nods from the crew and telephone calls of approval from the viewers. Feeling like a fraud—knowing that if it hadn't been for Dick and his team of technical geniuses the show would have been the disaster she deserved—she went home early, vowing to throw off this moodiness before the next morning.

But if anything, the next day was even worse. She found herself wandering around the station aimlessly, feeling too edgy and unsettled to concentrate on anything for more than a few minutes. To her credit, no one aside from the camera crew she took out to the zoo to tape a story about three new lion cubs seemed to notice anything unusual about her behavior. They had worked with her too often to be particularly concerned about the fact that she seemed oddly distracted. As good at their jobs as she usually was at hers, they teased her delightedly every time she flubbed her lines or missed a cue, then patiently compensated for her gaffes and wrapped up the taping early.

The floor crew was equally patient with her that evening. Dick and his technical director covered when she looked into the wrong camera. The production assistant compensated when she missed Mike Szaski's hand signals and ran overlong, messing up his precisely timed script and throwing the entire show off schedule. Even Gary "Buckshot" Garcia, the video tech, didn't howl in justifiable anguish when she appeared on the set in a snowy-white blouse that drove the signal levels from the cameras wild and kept his fingers dancing over his control board as he fought to keep the picture stable and color-correct.

Finally, it was over. She apologized profusely to everyone and crept home, subdued and downcast, wondering what on earth was happening to her. She was a professional, damn it! And professionals didn't act like this. Tomorrow, she vowed. Tomorrow would be better.

But later that night, alone with her own troubled thoughts, she finally admitted what the problem was. In fact, she realized wearily as she sank gratefully into a tub of steaming hot water, it could be neatly summed up in two words.

Logan Wilde.

For some reason, she'd almost managed to convince herself that he was going to call. She had been tied up in knots for two solid days now, jumping like a startled cat each time the telephone rang, holding her breath when she answered it only to have her heart sink when someone else's voice replied. But he hadn't called. And he wouldn't.

The other night had simply been a casual interlude to him, and it was time she admitted it and got all these silly fantasies out of her head. After all, she hadn't exactly been seduced. She had chosen to share his bed of her own volition, expecting nothing more than what he was offering for the moment. He hadn't swept her off her feet with pretty lies that night, hadn't made any false promises of everlasting love or long-term relationships. It had been just what it was: one of those magical, unplanned fantasies that happens once in a lifetime, cherished but never repeated. He'd obviously understood that right from the beginning. And it was time she came to terms with it and got on with her life.

She sank into the hot scented water and tried not to think of that other tub, of the hard, lean male body that had shared it with her. With her eyes closed, it took no effort at all to imagine that she was back in his penthouse apartment, that the silken touch of her bath sponge was his cheek against hers, the hot musky scent of bath oil his cologne.

Something patted her wet cheek. Cassidy sat upright with a startled gasp, spraying hot soapy water over the inquisitive cat sitting beside her. Sam scrambled off the edge of the tub with an outraged meow, shaking herself furiously as she fled the added indignity of Cassidy's laughter.

"Sam, I'm sorry!" Cassidy called contritely.

But Sam had obviously had enough and stayed safely out of sight. Cassidy relaxed back into the hot water with another sigh.

"Blame Logan Wilde," she muttered to the invisible cat. "God knows, he's to blame for just about everything else that's gone wrong in my life lately."

Put him out of your mind, she told herself impatiently. You were just another woman passing through his life, loved tenderly and well while you were there but undoubtedly forgotten by now in the delights of another. Remember him for what he gave you, not for what you can't have. And for heaven's sake, stop brooding over him like a lovesick adolescent!

A week later, Cassidy had all but managed to keep her resolve to forget Logan Wilde. Every now and again something would remind her of his gritty laugh, of the way his mouth would turn up so irresistibly in that lazy, teasing smile. But she managed to catch those renegade thoughts promptly and banish them from her mind, and by Friday afternoon, to everyone's relief including her own, everything was more or less back to normal.

She sailed through *Headliners* like a pro and was pulling on her jacket to go home when Ken Vaughn caught up with her.

He was frowning. "Cassidy, I need a favor."

Cassidy gave him a sharp look. Things had been decidedly cool between them all week, and she was frankly surprised to see him down on the floor at all.

He must have seen some of this in her eyes because he swore softly, running his hand through his hair. "Look, Cass," he said quietly, "I know I've been giving you a hard time this week."

"I don't know why you think that," she said agreeably. "Aside from cancelling my Taos special five minutes before it went on-air, and shooting down every single idea I've brought up at the morning planning meetings."

"I know, I know," he replied wearily. Then he smiled. "How would you like another chance to get that Taos show aired?"

Cassidy looked at him for a long while. Then she gave a quiet laugh and walked toward the door, shaking her head. "No deal. I'm not going to compromise myself or my work like that. I either make it in this business on talent, Ken, or I don't make it at all. I'm not selling out again."

Ken laughed. "Idealistic to the bitter end! All right—no games, no deals. I need someone to cover that hot air balloon rally this weekend."

Cassidy paused, one hand already on the door knob. "I thought Marsh was handling it."

"He was. But he's decided that doing a hot air balloon promo for a chronic care hospital isn't dignified enough for a man of his professional stature."

Cassidy looked at Ken closely. She'd never heard such sarcastic anger in his voice before and wondered if Marsh's abrasiveness was finally starting to wear him down.

"So," he continued with a sigh, "we're short one real live TV personality. The news boys can fly our balloon, but they're not going to draw much of an audience. The other stations are all sending in their big guns, and Crothers is real intent on making sure we do everything we can to make this rally a success."

Cassidy's first reaction was to tell Ken quite cheerfully to drop dead, but she resisted it. Waging war with the executive producer was one sure way to commit professional suicide, and the constant friction between them was starting to affect station morale. And besides, she mused, it might be fun. "All right."

Relief washed over Ken's features. "I owe you, Cass! Someone will pick you up Saturday morning. Talk to Tex McGuire in News and arrange it. We'll have lots of camera crews on hand, by the way, so take someone up with you and give us a minute-by-minute."

"Up?" Cassidy echoed, enthusiasm instantly waning. "You didn't tell me I had to go *up* in one of them. I thought you were just looking for someone to represent the station. On the ground."

"Didn't I mention that?" Ken looked at her innocently. "Well, don't worry about it. Just hang on tight and don't look down. You'll do just fine. Trust me."

"Just hang on tight and don't look down," Tex McGuire teased as he wrestled the wheel of the four-wheel-drive Suburban. "You'll be fine, Cass, honey. Trust me!"

Cassidy gave the tall, lean-faced Texan an eloquent look, clinging desperately to the door frame with one hand and Jackson dePaul's denim clad arm with the other as the Suburban bucked down the dusty, washboard road.

"This your first time in a balloon?" Jackson shouted over the roar of the engine.

"Yes, if I live long enough to get out to the rally! Does he always drive like this?"

"Yep!" Jackson replied happily. "When you're in the news department, you learn to drive like hell to beat everybody else to a story." He gave her a huge grin. "You're riding with the top news team in New Mexico, baby. We don't come in second to anybody!"

"I can believe that!" Cassidy gave a yelp as the Suburban hit a bump and sailed into the air. Jackson pulled her into his lap to steady her, although Cassidy suspected that he was enjoying it just a little too much. She extricated herself from his helpful grip, shooting Tex a glare that made him grin all the wider.

"Why don't you give up all that *Headliners* stuff and come work with us?" he asked.

"I do!" Cassidy reminded him. "Who reads your stuff on the air twice a day?"

He gave a snort. "Any damn fool can read what's handed to them," he told her bluntly. "You do top-notch work, kid. But you're wasting yourself playing comedy relief to Wheeler and reading a prewritten news report twice a day. I've never been able to figure out why you don't tell Vaughn to drop dead, and come on over to News to do some honest work for a change."

"We'd make a hell of a team, Cass!" Jackson put in. "I saw some of the rough cuts on that Taos water program you did—fantastic stuff! How come it never aired?"

"Politics. Fifth floor thought it was too touchy."

"You mean Marsh Wheeler thought it was too touchy," Tex corrected.

"Marsh? He didn't have anything to do with it."

Jackson and Tex exchanged a fleeting glance. "The fifth floor mortgaged their souls to get Wheeler to join KALB," Jackson said. "They figured the station needed one big name to bring in the viewers. But word's out the tail's wagging the dog. That Wheeler's blackmailing them into doing things his way by threatening to quit."

"I've been hearing that ever since I came out here," Cassidy said impatiently. "And I don't believe it."

"I saw those rough cuts, too." Tex put in, hard blue eyes narrowed on the road. "The little I saw was better than anything KALB's aired since we started up three years ago. And I'm damn certain no one's more aware of that than Wheeler."

Cassidy looked at Tex, frowning. "I'm flattered that you think I'm good enough to make an old pro like Marsh Wheeler nervous, but I think you're—oh!"

Tex gave a rebel yell as the Surburban shot into the air.

Cassidy's elbow smashed into the door handle, bringing tears to her eyes and putting a succinct end to her defense of Marsh Wheeler. Jackson held onto her and she clutched at him gratefully, not even minding his familiarity as a strong, tanned arm settled comfortably around her waist. "Do you guys do this a lot?" she asked breathlessly.

"Every chance we get!" Jackson assured her, pulling her solidly against him as the Suburban bounced over a pothole. "Just think of the fun you'd have if you came over to News."

"I doubt I'd survive the first week," she told him laughingly. "But I meant, do you go ballooning often?"

"As often as work and weather allow." Tex gave his head a nod toward the back of the Suburban. "Bought our own rig about a year ago. A bunch of us get together once or twice a week. If the weather's okay, we go up; if it isn't, we drink beer and swap lies. Albuquerque's the hot air balloon capital of the world, so there's always something going on: races, Hare and Hounds, Tied Ribbon Fly—" He stopped, seeing her expression. "You know much about balloons?"

"Only that they go up. And, with luck, stay there."

Minutes later, Tex pulled the Suburban abruptly off the road and into what looked like open desert. Bruised and dusty, ribs aching from where Jackson's arm had been holding her, Cassidy brushed her tousled hair from her face and peered out the windshield. As the dust cleared, she saw what looked like a Gypsy encampment spread out ahead of them.

Numerous dust coated, battered vehicles were parked here and there, disgorging equipment and people. Television camera vans were parked tidily to one side. One was already set up for a live broadcast, spewing thick cables and electrical equipment. Two men were standing nearby drinking coffee, one with a heavy camera perched on his shoulder. They glanced up curiously as Tex gave them a raucous blast of the horn. One of them waved and the other, hands cupping his mouth, shouted something that Cassidy didn't quite catch.

"Oh, look!" Cassidy pointed to where a giant balloon had blossomed into life. It hung in the air as delicately as thistledown, its brilliant colors breathtakingly vibrant in the early morning sun. Tugging lightly at the ropes tethering it, it seemed almost alive, like some giant land-bound bird straining anxiously toward the freedom of the sky.

Jackson laughed quietly. "Just wait'll you see a dozen or more lift off at the same time like a flock of overweight flamingos!"

Cassidy gave a delighted laugh as Tex pulled the Suburban to a spine-jarring stop. Jackson turned to peer out the rear window. "Hardy and the others follow us okay?"

"Right behind us," Tex said just as the cobalt-blue KALB News van appeared out of the cloud of dust veiling the highway. "How are we gonna do this? Hardy's never been up in a balloon either.

"You take Hardy up with you," Jackson said promptly as the three of them got out of the Suburban. He smiled at Cassidy. "I'm going to show Cass here all there is to know about hot air ballooning."

"He's right about the hot air part, anyway," Tex drawled, giving Cassidy a wink. "If he brings you down in a romantic little spot and says he's run out of gas, send up a flare and I'll come and rescue you."

Cassidy laughed, glad that Marsh had changed his mind about taking part in the promotional rally. She had always suspected that the News Department had all the fun!

"Hey, if it isn't Cassidy Yorke, the prettiest face on Albuquerque television—with the exception of my own, of course." Cassidy looked around and found herself staring up into the handsome features of Tim O'Hagan, the sports announcer for KALB's chief competitor. "When are you going to quit this sorry excuse for a television station and come work for a *real* station, Cass?"

"Probably about the same time you go back to pro football, O'Hagan," Tex drawled. "Which is never, considering you play ball as bad as you announce it."

"I'm serious," Tim went on, unfazed by the sarcasm. "We'd hire you away from these turkeys in a minute. Give you twice the bucks, your own show. Just think—no more zoo shots, no more Marsh Wheeler, no more of these two clowns . . ."

Cassidy laughed, wondering what he would do if she took him up on the offer on the spot.

"Cassidy Yorke! Glad you made it!" Milt Cordova, one of KALB's senior executives, was striding toward her. He eyed her casual white cotton playsuit, sandals and loosely gathered ponytail with frank approval. "There's going to be a pre-race press conference with the mayor, representatives from the Hutcheson, and all the celebrity participants, Cassidy. It'll be going out live over the networks for the nine o'clock news, so don't forget to put on fresh lipstick and your prettiest smile."

Cassidy bristled, but Tex was suddenly there, stepping smoothly between them. He gave Cassidy a surreptitious wink. "We'll get our own cameras set up for a direct feed and have it on-air locally before the networks get it."

"Good idea!" Cordova nodded emphatically, smiling at Cassidy. "With lots of coverage of our favorite celebrity here, of course. Come on over, Cassidy, and I'll introduce you to everyone."

As she walked silently beside Cordova, Cassidy reminded herself that he wasn't being deliberately offensive. The truth was that television was still very much a man's field, in spite of the inroads made by women. She slipped Cordova an irritated glance. And it was men like him who helped keep her on the "zoo circuit" while the serious interviews went to Marsh.

The rally organizers had built a small canopied platform on which to display their guest celebrities and sponsors. It was already ringed by television cameras, and she and Cordova had to make their way gingerly through winding cables and dangling boom microphones. The mayor was there, shaking hands with someone Cassidy recognized as an aide to the Governor. She recognized some of the others: a well-known golf pro now living in Albuquerque, a statuesque *Playboy* centerfold, a smattering of media personalities like herself, a couple of local businessmen, even a politician or two.

She sensed more than heard someone come up behind her. She turned, smiling. And froze, staring speechlessly up into those oh-so-familiar cobalt-blue eyes. They held hers for what seemed like an eternity, mirroring a surprise almost as great as her own.

"Miss Yorke." Logan Wilde smiled warily. "I didn't expect to see you here."

Cassidy finally managed to get her breath back. She held out her hand. "Hello, Logan."

Six

Logan's hand wrapped around hers gently. "How are you, Cassidy?"

So formal, she thought. So cool. They could have been casual business acquaintances trading social niceties at a once a year sales convention. In spite of herself, she thought of the wild, uninhibited lovemaking she'd shared with this man. And suddenly she realized the question wasn't quite as cool as it sounded. He was thinking of that night, too. And the anger and bitterness afterward. Hand still in his, she smiled. "I'm fine, Logan," she assured him softly. "And you?"

"I'm all right, Cass." He said it quietly, privately, as though the babble and confusion around them didn't exist. Their eyes seemed to lock. For an instant, his public mask fell away and it was the other Logan Wilde standing there: the loving, gentle one she had fallen half in love with the other night. His gaze searched hers, as though seeking the answer to some important question.

"Logan! Oh, Mr. Wilde, look over here!" Camera flashes went off like firecrackers. A group of giggling women crowded around the bottom of the platform, elbowing each other aside for a better shot. Abruptly, the public mask slid into place. He smiled down at them patiently.

"Hey, Cassidy! Cassidy Yorke!" A reporter from one of KALB's competitors, video camera poised, shouldered his way to the front. "Hey, honey, how was your date with Wilde the other night? You sure didn't give much away on your show."

Logan laughed and draped his arm around her shoulders. "You should never put a lady on the spot like that," he drawled into the camera.

"Aw, come on!" someone else protested. "What was it like, Cassidy? Come on, honey. Ten million women out there are dying to know!"

Cassidy smiled into the camera. "Let's just say that the evening was everything I expected it to be."

The first man gave a whoop. "Does that mean he's everything he says he is? Come on, hon—tell us. The public has a right to know."

Cassidy gritted her teeth, fighting a growing urge to throw something at the man. She forced herself to laugh gaily. "Oh, Logan Wilde is everything he says he is. And more!"

"Yeah, but—"

"Hey, you guys," Logan protested laughingly. "Give the lady a break!"

"What about her, Logan? Answer the question that every man in New Mexico's been asking himself for the past year. What's Cassidy Yorke *really* like?"

"Cassidy Yorke is the kind of woman fantasies are made of," he purred. "And I'm taking the Fifth on anything beyond that, gentlemen."

He was working them as skillfully as any country fair huckster, Cassidy realized, giving them exactly what they wanted while not relinquishing a thing, being the man they wanted him to be for the moment. With another crowd, at another moment, he would be someone else again, blending with his audience's expectations like a chameleon. He'd done the same thing with her, being the man she needed at the time, letting her think she was getting more of him than he was really giving. She thought of the information in the press kit, of the numerous articles written about him, of the radio and television appearances. Smoke and mirrors, she mused. Like Wilde himself, they seemed to be solid enough, until you tried to grab them, and then they simply drifted between your fingers, tenuous as mist.

She watched him as he deftly fielded more questions and suddenly realized just how little she really knew this man. They had made love, yet he was as much a stranger to her as he was to these reporters. For that matter, did anyone know him? Cradled in the curve of his arm, feeling his body warmth, breathing in the musky scent of him, she had the uneasy feeling that he wasn't really there at all. That if she put her hand out it would simply go through him as it would go through an image reflected on water. *Was* there really a man called Logan Wilde, she found herself wondering. Or was he as much an illusion to himself as he was to everyone else? Suddenly she thought of something he'd told her the other night: *every time you sell out, you sell a bit more of yourself.* Had that happened to him, she wondered. Had he given so much of himself away that there was nothing left but a mockery of what had once been real?

"Kiss her, Logan! Come on, you two. Give us a shot!"

But before they could respond, to Cassidy's intense relief, Milt Cordova had insinuated himself between them. Draping an arm around each of them, he smiled widely into the cameras. "That's enough, now, boys," he told the reporters and television newsmen. "We've got a balloon rally to get off the ground."

The next hour was a blur to Cassidy. She shook hands and smiled until her face ached, murmured words to this official or that, listened to a half dozen speeches by people she had never heard of before. But through it all she was aware of nothing but Logan Wilde.

He seemed as uncomfortable with her presence as she was with his. Neither of them said more than a dozen words to each other, and every time their eyes met, his seemed a little more troubled. But finally the last hand was shaken, the last picture taken. Cassidy kept her gaze resolutely from Logan's as everyone left the platform and started across to where the balloons were being readied for the start of the race. A handful of representatives from the Hutcheson clinic was there, looking slightly overwhelmed and self-conscious.

The exception was the clinic's director, Dr. Katherine Salazar, a tall, attractive woman with short steel-gray hair and an air of no-nonsense competence about her. She had clasped Cassidy's hand firmly when they'd been introduced, her smile reserved, sharp gray eyes unnervingly direct. When she'd thanked Cassidy for donating her time and support to the clinic, Cassidy got the impression that although the words were sincere enough, Dr. Salazar was all too aware that Cassidy, like the rest of KALB, was there as much for the station's publicity as she was for the clinic's. Cassidy had taken an instant liking to her. She was watching one of the giant balloons being inflated now, her face as filled with delight as a child's.

She looked around as Cassidy and Cordova approached. "It looks like marvelous fun, Milt! Are you going up?"

"Cassidy here's our celebrity balloonist, not me!" He patted Cassidy's shoulder.

Salazar speared Cassidy with those piercing sleet-gray eyes. "Have you been out to our facility, Miss Yorke?" When Cassidy replied that she hadn't, Salazar nodded again. "Come out sometime and have a look around." Her mouth lifted with a faint smile. "And bring a cameraman. God knows, we could use the publicity."

"That's not a half bad idea, actually." Cassidy glanced at Cordova.

An expression of fleeting impatience crossed Cordova's face. "Well, yes, it has possibilitites . . ."

Liar, Cassidy thought to herself. You're no more going to mention it to Crothers than fly that balloon! We'll all stand here and smile our false smiles and make the appropriate noises, and by tomorrow the Hutcheson clinic and Katherine Salazar will have been forgotten. Salazar's shrewd glance brushed hers as though by accident and Cassidy saw the weary disbelief in her eyes, as though she'd heard all the meaningless promises before and no more believed that Cassidy would come out to the clinic than Cassidy believed it herself. Cassidy looked away, ashamed of Cordova's lies and her own helplessness.

"Hey, Cass! We're ready to inflate."

Cassidy peered through the gathering crowd of bystanders. She finally caught sight of Tex's tall, lanky form and gave him a wave of acknowledgment, then turned to Salazar. "Wish me luck!"

"I wish I were coming with you." Salazar smiled wistfully. "But I'm supposed to greet the winner at the finishing line with the traditional champagne toast. I'll be up there with you in spirit, though, and good luck!"

Cassidy turned to give Salazar and Cordova a quick wave as she worked her way through the crowd to where the dozen or so balloons were being readied for flight. Most had already been pulled out of their protective canvas bags, and the brightly colored nylon canopies lay stretched out on the ground, downwind from their wicker gondola baskets.

The teams of men and women worked with a quick, earnest efficiency. Everyone seemed to know everyone else and there was a good deal of good-natured joking back and forth between the teams. Tex and Jackson were just finishing bolting together the support frame for the burners and hooking up the fuel lines that ran from the propane tanks to the burner.

"This is the *Phoenix*, KALB's official entry," Tex told her. "You and Jackson will go up in her." He gave his head a nod toward another balloon stretched out beside them. "That's the *Fire Eagle*. I'm taking Hardy and his camera up. After we get good elevation, we'll keep them side by side for as long as possible so Hardy can get some good shots of you and *Phoenix* to tie in with your commentary." He looked at Jackson, grinning broadly. "Then it's every man for himself!"

"I'll have Cass over the finish line and in the pub before the rest of you guys figure out which way you're going," Jackson promised.

There was a squeal of female laughter behind her and Cassidy glanced around curiously. A handful of television and newspaper reporters were milling around excitedly, shouting questions into apparent thin air. Then the crush parted and Cassidy saw the cause of all the excitement.

She was beautiful, there was no denying that, Cassidy admitted grudgingly. Miss March—or was it April?—laughed breathlessly into the cameras, a confection of wide blue eyes and glowing skin and shimmering blond hair. Wearing a silver lamé jumpsuit that emphasized every spectacular curve, she was obviously enjoying the ardent attention she was receiving. And standing beside her, one arm draped casually around that improbably slender waist, looking incredibly handsome and just slightly bored as he smiled lazily into the cameras, was Logan Wilde.

Of course, Cassidy thought to herself with a stab of sudden and totally unreasonable anger. Who else would escort the luscious Miss April or whatever to the finish line? She shoved her hands into the pockets of her playsuit, unable to take her eyes off them. They made a spectacular couple, no doubt about it. Both tall and lean and well tanned, they could have stepped off the set of a Hollywood movie. Logan's dark good looks complemented his partner's blond beauty perfectly, although his tight white jeans, matching denim bomber jacket and colorful western-cut shirt made her look slightly overdressed. Of course, thought Cassidy a trifle maliciously, considering what she was used to wearing, Miss April would be overdressed in a fig leaf!

Logan glanced up unexpectedly and his gaze met Cassidy's for a split second. Then one of the reporters shouted something and Logan looked away, smiling as he posed for yet another shot. Miss April snuggled into the curve of his arm and Cassidy turned away abruptly, wondering with sudden and savage anger why she had ever let Ken Vaughn talk her into this stupid rally in the first place.

Tex and Jackson were filling the balloon envelope with air now. Slowly, the long ribbon of bright nylon started to take life. Its glossy skin rippled and one of the ground crew held a rope attached to the top of the envelope, watching to ensure that a sudden gust of wind didn't catch it and roll it, twisting the cables holding the basket. On either side, more and more balloons started taking shape. They were like fairytale monsters waking from winter's hibernation, taking deep breaths of air and flexing their muscles before taking flight. Slowly, they lost their long, fat sausage shapes and started looking like balloons. They stirred restlessly in the light breeze. Excitement ran through Cassidy, and she slipped under the rope barricade to join her two compatriots.

Tex smiled at her. "Ready? Got your tape recorder?"

Cassidy patted her shoulder bag. "Right here. Are we almost ready to go up?"

"Just a final check or two, then we light the burners."

Cassidy stood beside them, her excitement growing as she watched the balloon fill. Behind her, Miss April laughed musically. Cassidy ignored it. The balloon was about three-quarters inflated by now, lying lazily on its side. Frowning with concentration, Tex adjusted something on the burner nozzle. There was a sudden, incredibly loud roar of sound and a long blue flame gouted into the gaping mouth of the balloon. Cassidy jumped, badly startled, feeling a little silly when she realized what was happening.

Jackson grinned. "It'll take a couple of minutes."

Nodding, Cassidy watched the balloon avidly. Finally, after what seemed like an impossibly long while, it started to lift, almost imperceptibly. Tex worked the blast valve, sending short, regular gouts of heat into the envelope.

"It takes fifteen, maybe twenty seconds before she responds to the extra heat," Jackson explained.

"Is that the only control you have?"

"Basically, yes. There's a maneuvering slit there on the side, about halfway up. See the cord leading back to the basket? Pull it, and hot air's vented for descent. You can control your vertical travel pretty closely just with the burner—more heat and she rises, less and she comes down. Past that it's skill and luck—skill at reading the wind currents, luck in finding the right one to give you the direction and speed you want."

Delicately, the balloon started to lift upright, as majestic as an ocean liner. All around them other balloons started doing the same, seeming to grow out of the ground like giant mushrooms. Jackson motioned her to come closer and Cassidy stared up into the balloon. It was huge, divided into segments like an orange. Sunlight filtered through the blue and red fabric and Cassidy thought of a circus tent. She stepped back and stared up at it, realizing for the first time that a black, stylized phoenix had been painted on the side, wings spreading as the balloon inflated. It tugged at the tethering ropes, straining toward the empty blue sky.

"First time up?"

Cassidy looked around. Logan smiled down at her. "Yes," she replied. "And you?"

Jackson gave a snort of laughter. "Logan's one of the top balloonists in the state. He's been racing them—and winning—for a couple of years now."

"Really?" Cassidy looked up at him with renewed curiosity. "I didn't know that."

"There's a hell of a lot you don't know about me," he drawled, sky-blue eyes holding hers with disarming boldness. "In spite of . . . everything."

It was the truth. Cassidy felt her cheeks turn a delicate pink and she tore her gaze from his, pretending to watch the balloon. "Well, good luck. You ought to have an interesting flight. I'm sure Miss April will be great company."

"Miss May," he corrected benignly, staring up at the balloon. "Actually, I was thinking about changing partners."

"Really?" She slid him a droll look. "I thought you made an adorable couple. Blonde looks very good on you."

"I prefer brunettes." He turned his head to look down at her. "Small, bad-tempered brunettes with green eyes are a particular weakness."

Cassidy pretended not to know what he was talking about. She wondered why her pulse was racing as she leaned toward Jackson, shouting to be heard over the ripping roar of the burner. "Are we just about ready?"

"There goes the test balloon." Jackson pointed skyward. Cassidy could see a tiny child's balloon bobbing upward.

The burner shut off. In the sudden silence, Cassidy could hear other burners pulsing on and off around them, blending with happy laughter and shouts of encouragement and advice from the onlookers.

"Okay, Cass, hop in."

"Change in plan," Logan said from behind her. "Miss Yorke's coming with me."

"What?" Cassidy looked around in confusion. "What are you—Logan!" Before she realized what he was doing, Logan had picked her up in his arms. "Logan, you can't—"

"You don't mind taking up Miss May, do you?" Logan asked Jackson calmly, ignoring Cassidy's sputtered protests and struggles.

Jackson looked mildly dazed as Miss May walked toward them. She looked decidedly displeased with the new arrangement, her blue eyes frigid as she glared at Logan. "I thought *I* was going up with you."

"Jackson dePaul works for one of the local television stations, honey," Logan told her as he strode by, holding Cassidy firmly as she tried to squirm free.

At the magic word *television*, Miss May's sulky pout vanished. Eyes widening, she slipped her arm into Jackson's and leaned lightly against him, smiling up into his dazed, smiling face.

"Logan, damn it, put me down!"

"Quit wriggling. And don't swear. It's not ladylike."

Cassidy gave an outraged sputter.

Calmly, Logan dumped her into the basket of his balloon. A knot of photographers who had been wandering around taking random shots of the activities suddenly converged on them, shouting questions. Logan smiled his very best public smile and stepped into the basket, tidily trapping Cassidy between him and one of his ground crew, who was working the blast value on the burner. He murmured something to the other man, who nodded and stepped out of the basket. What in heaven's name was going on, she fumed, trying to squeeze past Logan without touching the burner.

Logan took control of the burner, still smiling broadly at the reporters and photographers. "Smile, darling," he murmured. "You're going to be on the front page of half the newspapers in the country by tonight." Then, not even turning his head, he shouted, "Let'er go!"

Cassidy saw her chance. Clasping one of the support cables, she was just about to clamber out of the basket when it suddenly trembled and tipped slightly to one side. Snatching at the padded edge of the basket for balance, she looked around in alarm as the crowd started to move.

"I wouldn't get out just now if I were you," Logan suggested in that calm, laughing voice.

"Logan?" She tightened her grip on the basket edge as, delicate as smoke, they started to rise. "Lo—oh, my God!"

Cassidy held her breath as the ground dropped away from them. There was no sensation of rising. Instead, it was as if they had discarded the confining bulk of the earth itself. She watched it fall away with a sense of awe, the trucks and waving onlookers growing smaller and smaller until they looked like a child's toys.

"Oh... wow!" she whispered, taking a deep breath and unknotting her fingers from the basket. She looked up. The massive bulk of the balloon envelope blotted out all but a tiny crescent of sky as it bore them gently upward. It was utterly silent. They were moving with the wind so the air was as still and silken as glass, and Cassidy could hear the creak of the woven reed basket, a distant birdsong, even the faint growl of truck engines as, far below them, the ground crews took up the chase.

A hiss broke the stillness, so loud that Cassidy's heart very nearly stopped until she remembered where she was. And why. She turned around and glared at Logan. "Do you always have to do that?"

"Yes," he replied quite innocently. "The flame heats the air inside the canopy, which in turn creates the lift that—"

"Not the gas, damn it, that song and dance with the reporters!"

"What song and dance?"

"That whole scene down there. Picking me up and carrying me off like the spoils of war. Turning it into a big event. Why do you always play up to them like that?"

Logan gave the valve a brief twist. The flame shot up, blue as hot steel. After a second or two he shut it off again. "What makes you think it was for the media?"

"Wasn't it?" She gave her head a toss. "They ate it up, as usual. Playboy Logan Wilde playing his role to the hilt."

"Just part of the image," he reminded her coolly.

"Well, I don't like that image," she advised him just as coolly. "And I'd appreciate it if you'd stick to your calendar pinups and leave me out of it."

Logan's expression darkened. "I play their games when the payoff is right."

"And just what was the payoff this time?" she demanded frostily. "Front page coverage from coast to coast?"

"No." He stared at her. "You."

He turned his attention back to the balloon. Caught off guard, Cassidy stared at him. "I didn't think you wanted to see me again," she said after a while, slightly subdued.

"I didn't." He gave the balloon another brief blast of flame, not looking at her. "Then I saw you today and changed my mind."

"Oh." It seemed like an inadequate reply, but for the life of her Cassidy didn't know what to say. Balloons dotted the bright blue New Mexican sky around them like rainbow confetti, some higher, some lower, all seeming to hang motionless while the earth grew smaller beneath them. She could hear distant voices and shouts of laughter and the intermittent snarl of gas jets.

"Like to try your hand at this?"

She looked around at him. He held her gaze steadily and after a moment she eased around beside him with an inward sigh. What an enigma this man was: Logan Wilde one moment, a complete stranger the next. Surely he hadn't kidnapped her just to show her how to pilot a balloon.

"It takes a few seconds to get a response," he explained. "After a while you get a feel for it, judging how much to give her and when."

Cassidy put her hand tentatively on the valve. Gingerly, she opened it. Blue fire blazed and she winced, gazing nervously upward. Nothing happened. She glanced at Logan.

He smiled. "Wait for it."

"How can you tell if we're moving or not?"

"Take a fix on something—that yellow truck following us down there."

She did as he told her, her heart giving a little leap of excitement when the truck suddenly seemed to recede as the balloon responded to the heated air. She laughed with delight, thrilled as the balloon obeyed her slightest command, moving obediently up or down as she opened and closed the valve. Their shadow followed them, racing to keep up as it scrambled over the rocky terrain below. It swelled when they moved lower, and dwindled to inconsequence when they rose.

"Oh, Logan, it's absolutely fantastic!" Laughing, she brushed her tangled hair from her eyes. "I never want to go down!"

"I kind of felt that way when we were making love."

She looked at him, startled. A warm blush tinted her cheeks and she looked down, suddenly unable to meet his eyes. "I—I felt the same way."

He was so silent that after a moment she finally dared to look at him. He was staring down at her with pensive eyes. Then, still saying nothing, he reached across and turned the valve full on, letting the flame roar for a long while. Silently, the balloon lifted, rising higher and higher. It turned slowly with a shift in the wind currents, giving them a different perspective of mountains and plains and companion balloons.

"That should hold us for a minute or two," he said. "Or long enough, anyway."

"Long enough?"

"To kiss you. Properly." He leaned forward and slipped his hands around her waist, drawing her toward him.

His mouth covered hers, his kiss intimate and warm and deeply probing. Cassidy closed her eyes and relaxed against him, holding nothing back, feeling her body blossom vibrantly in response to the erotically familiar taste of him.

"Oh, Cassie," he moaned, giving her a fierce hug. "This has been the longest week of my life!"

"I thought you'd call," she admitted shyly.

"God, I did! A few thousand times. But for the life of me I couldn't figure out what to say to you, so I'd hang up before it rang."

"You wouldn't have had to say anything," she murmured candidly. "Just knowing you cared enough to call would have been enough. I would have known the rest."

He buried his face in her hair, sighing contentedly. "I couldn't believe it when I turned around today and saw you. It was like I was being given a second chance—except you seemed so cool, so distant. I nearly convinced myself that you just wanted to forget that whole evening. Then I decided to hell with it, I had to make a move. If you told me to drop dead, fine. At least I'd know for certain then." He eased her away from him, staring down at her. "But I had to find out how you felt, Cass. That night with you was too special to let go. *You're* too special to let go."

Cassidy held his gaze evenly. "Logan," she said quietly, "did you ask me out that night and sleep with me because of the challenge? Or because . . . because . . ." She faltered, suddenly not quite knowing how to go on.

"Partly," he admitted bluntly. "I did invite you out to prove a point. I had every intention of going just far enough to make it a foregone conclusion that you'd stay the night—then tossing you out on your gorgeous backside." He looked down at her steadily. "But something happened that night, Cass. For a while it wasn't Logan Wilde, *lover extraordinaire*, and Cassidy Yorke, wonder-child of the networks, up there. It was just you and me and some magic I don't even know how to explain. I made love to you that night because you're the most exciting, captivating woman I've met in years." He paused, frowning. "I overreacted that night. You hit a sensitive spot, and I lashed out without even thinking about what I was saying. That's a pretty damn poor excuse for an apology, I know, but I don't know what else to say." He took another deep breath. "The truth is, I get a lot of women passing through my life who want nothing more from me than a few hours in my bed. Sometimes they're just curious, sometimes they want to be able to say they've slept with the famous Logan Wilde." His mouth curved in a self-mocking smile. "Apparently I'm quite a coup."

"I'm not interested in collecting scalps, Logan," Cassidy told him quietly. "I started out that evening not liking you very much. I was pretty sure you intended to try to get me into bed, just to teach me a lesson for giving you a hard time on my show, and I fully intended to lead you in a merry circle to get the material I wanted. Then I was going to take my tape recorder, and my virtue, and calmly walk out of your life." She smiled dryly. "So much for well-laid plans."

Logan winced. "You must have decided you'd been right about me when I didn't call. That you'd been . . . used."

Cassidy's smile widened. "You hardly dragged me into your bed kicking and screaming, Logan. You asked me if I was sure, remember. I was. And I still am. No regrets."

He seemed to relax, and he smiled as he reached for her. "Come here and tell me that again."

Laughing softly, Cassidy slipped into his embrace. "I hope Eric Hardy doesn't have a long lens on that camera of his, or we could be the highlight of the six o'clock news."

"To hell with them," he growled, mouth seeking hers hungrily. "I'm tired of television cameras and radio talk shows and autograph sessions and the pretty, empty-headed women everyone seems to think I favor. Now shut up and kiss me."

"Bully!" Cassidy said teasingly against his mouth, then proceeded to do just that. His tongue circled hers with slow, rhythmic intensity, and he gave a soft groan of pleasure as she guided it more deeply into her mouth. His hands slid the full length of her back, pressing her against him. They curled around the lush curve of her bottom, lifting and molding her to him, boldly showing her just how vitally his own body was responding to those unspoken memories of what they'd shared.

"Oh, my God, Cassie!" he gasped, tearing his mouth from hers to nuzzle her throat. "I've been going out of my mind! Your perfume's still in my bed and I lie awake half the night, remembering the feel and taste of you, seeing you naked and wet in my arms, remembering the way you moved, the way you touched me . . ." His mouth found hers again and he kissed her urgently, almost roughly. "I turn that damned television on at nine in the morning and leave it on all day just so I won't miss one of your newscasts. Every time I hear your voice, every time you look into the camera and your eyes meet mine, something twists in my gut so hard it hurts. It's all I've been able to do to keep from storming into that studio and dragging you off into the night!"

"Logan . . ."

"I've never in my life wanted a woman the way I want you," Logan whispered fiercely.

"Logan!" Panting, Cassidy tried to turn her mouth away from his. "Logan, the trees—!"

"What trees?" He went on kissing her throat, her ear. "Cass, don't turn away from me like this! I—"

"The trees we're going to hit in a minute if you don't get this balloon up fast!" she blurted out in one long rush, eyes widening as the mountain ledge loomed nearer, its tufted fringe of glossy pine trees getting larger by the instant.

Seven

"What?" Logan's head shot up. "Oh—!" His oath was earthy and heartfelt and Cassidy had to snatch at the burner frame for support as he thrust her away from him. Blue flame exploded upward and Cassidy stared at the nearing trees in fascinated horror.

"Up," Logan breathed urgently. "Come on, baby! Lift!"

Cassidy had to bite her lip from laughing at the sheer insanity of it, heart racing with exhilaration. She found herself chanting the words with Logan, *up up up*, not really believing they were going to clear the crest of trees yet feeling absolutely no fear. It was too beautiful to be dangerous. The ancient, wind twisted trees etched a lacy filigree of green against the sky ahead of them, and the air was filled with their spicy scent. The roar of the flame stilled abruptly and in the sudden silence she could hear the surf sound of wind in tree boughs and the stacatto scolding of a squirrel.

Slowly, almost imperceptibly at first, they started to rise. Then, swiftly, they shot up like a cork out of a bottle. The trees flashed by, the heavy green boughs seeming to stretch yearningly upward. The uppermost tuft of one old warrior actually scraped the bottom of the basket and Cassidy hung over the side, watching them fall away into the distance. She straightened, looking at Logan, and started to laugh.

He sagged against the side of the basket, staring at her in disbelief. Then he started to laugh too, reaching for her. "I've always heard that danger's an aphrodisiac," he murmured huskily, running his hands up and down her back. "All this fresh air and excitement's gone to my head."

Laughing, Cassidy lifted his questing hand from her breast. "As long as you're piloting this airship, good sir, I'll thank you to keep your hands on the appropriate equipment—the balloon's, not mine!" she amended hastily, catching his mischievous hand again. "I'd rather we maintained positive elevation or whatever you call it."

"Oh, we're maintaining positive elevation, my love," he assured her with a laugh. "Believe me, we're doing that!"

Cassidy gave him a look of tolerant disgust. "I hate to distract you from your letchery, but have you noticed that we've lost the rest of the pack?"

"Not quite," he corrected with a cheerful grin, nodding toward the horizon. It was dotted with tiny round bits of color, brilliant as chipped glass in the sun.

"We're never going to catch up! Quick, Logan, take her up—way up! Tex said the winds are stronger the higher you go."

"Competitive little rascal, aren't you? We could just take our time, you know."

Cassidy gave her head an impatient shake, staring at those tantalizing beads strung along the horizon. "No, no—if you don't go into something to win, there's no point in going in at all! Take it up, Logan! Maybe we can still overtake them!"

But they couldn't. In fact, within a few minutes Cassidy had lost sight of all but one of the tiny, distant balloons, and in another minute or two even it had disappeared. She searched the sky ahead intently, then finally gave up with a sigh. "Well," she muttered finally, "I guess that's that."

"Did it really mean that much to you?"

She stared out into the hard blue sky, then suddenly relaxed and gave a quiet laugh. "Not really. I just hate losing anything, that's all."

He smiled wryly. "So I noticed."

"I have three brothers—all older than I am. They made my life a misery while I was growing up, teasing and meddling and bossing me around. They were bigger and better at everything. I was the kid sister, too small to play with, always in the way." She smiled fondly. "The only way I could get anyone to pay any attention to me was to be better at everything. Dad always said I grew up with twice as much stubbornness as anyone else in the family."

"I feel sorry for those brothers of yours," Logan teased. "I'll bet you were a holy terror!"

Cassidy's mouth curved reminiscently. "I had my moments." She suddenly realized that they were slowly descending, and she peered out at the nearing scrub trees and rocks below.

"I'm bringing her down," Logan replied to her unspoken question. "We're short of fuel, and if we get much more off course our chase car will never find us. They were following us pretty well for a while there, then I lost them." He gave the sere landscape behind them a long, searching look. "I hope they were able to keep us in sight."

Cassidy looked out at the mountainous countryside below with growing respect. "And if they don't?"

Logan glanced around at her, grinning. "Then we camp out until they find us. Which, with luck, may not be for days."

"It gets cold up here at night," she protested, hoping he was teasing. "And there are snakes and spiders and things!"

"A woman with three older brothers shouldn't be worried about snakes and spiders and things," he reminded her.

"And I'm sure we can come up with a few ideas to keep warm."

"I can see the headlines now," she groaned. "KALB news anchor lost in mountains with notorious womanizer."

Landing a balloon, Cassidy soon discovered, was more complicated than launching one. The balloon was born to fly, and, like some long-caged bird tasting sky flight and freedom for the first time, it was less than cooperative about returning to earth. Logan became very businesslike and serious, telling her where to stand and what to hold on to, and more importantly, what *not* to hold on to. He worked the maneuvering line, bringing them in at a steady angle, clear of trees and outcrops of rock. The ground seemed to rush up at them and Cassidy felt a thrill of nervousness as for the first time she became aware of height and speed and the fragility of the delicate bubble above her.

"Hang on tight," Logan said suddenly. "And don't jump out until we're down and the balloon's collapsed. Without your weight, it could lift off again, and it could take me a mile or more before I can get her down. I don't want you wandering around out here by yourself."

Cassidy nodded, her mouth suddenly dry as she watched the rocky landscape rush toward her. It seemed much too rough, littered with huge boulders, stunted trees, and a creek bed. Then, before she expected it, the basket touched solid earth, much more gently than she'd anticipated. Logan seemed to be doing a dozen things at once and she caught a glimpse of a monstrous red and blue cloud descending, collapsing gently like some great dying jellyfish. Then the basket tipped onto its side. A hand smacked her gently on the backside, urging her out, and she crawled out ignominiously on her hands and knees.

Logan scrambled to keep the nylon skirt from touching the hot burner. "You okay?"

"I'm fine." Cassidy got to her feet, staggering slightly. The balloon lay stretched out like a beached whale and she looked at it sadly.

As though reading her mind, Logan laughed and wrapped his arm around her shoulders in a quick hug. "We'll go up again, don't worry."

Then came the hard work of deflating the balloon, "milking" the air out of it, and carefully rolling it up. When they were finished, Cassidy looked up at the bright, clear blue sky, finding it difficult to believe that minutes ago they'd been up there, soaring as lazily as the hawk that was now circling on widespread wings.

"How did you like it?"

"Words can't even come close." She came back to earth with a little shake of her head, smiling. "I remember one winter afternoon when Kevin—he's my oldest brother—and I decided to make a parachute out of binder twine and an old tarp that dad had covering the tractor. We rigged this thing up and I climbed onto his back and hung on for dear life, and Kevin took a running start and jumped out of the hayloft." She laughed aloud at the expression on Logan's face. "We landed in a snowdrift, all tangled up in binder twine and canvas, right in the midst of a half dozen terrified heifers and my mother's flock of prize ducks. After the dust settled, so to speak, we both got the spanking we deserved. But I never forgot that split second when we really were flying." She looked at the sky yearningly. Then she laughed again. "Just before we landed and I hit my mouth on the top of Kevin's head and knocked out two of my front teeth."

Logan gave a snort of laughter and put the knuckles of one hand under her chin, tipping her face up. He stared at her mouth studiously, turning her face this way and that. "Looks okay to me," he finally said very seriously. "But maybe we should check it out, just to be sure."

"It happened about nineteen years ago," she advised him dryly. "And I didn't hear any complaints a few nights ago."

Chuckling softly, he drew her into his arms. "Don't be difficult, Cassidy. Just come here and kiss me."

"Do you boss all your women around like this?" She settled into his embrace comfortably.

"I don't have any women," he murmured, bringing his mouth down over hers. "Not until now."

As always, his kiss was magic and champagne, sending her senses reeling giddily. There was something satisfyingly proprietory about the way his mouth claimed hers, as though he knew with absolute certainty that she had no more doubts than he about the rightness of it. She loved the taste of him, the feel of his strong arms around her, the way the crisp curls on his nape curled around her fingers as she ran them up into his hair. There was the same feeling of rightness to being in his arms as there had been that night in his apartment when their kisses had led so naturally into lovemaking. Was this what it was like to be in love, she found herself wondering dizzily as his hands molded her against his lean body.

"Oh, Cassie," he murmured. "In all my life, I've never met anyone quite like you! You've touched things inside me that I'd decided didn't exist anymore, things I thought I'd lost sometime during the past two years of games and lies and—" He stopped, realizing she was staring up at him curiously. He frowned slightly, his eyes caressing her features lovingly one by one. "Cass, there's something I want to tell you." Again he paused, frown deepening.

"Yes?" Her laughing voice was filled with anticipation.

"I..." His eyes held hers, as though trying to decide something. Then he suddenly gave a reckless laugh, mood changing, and picked her up in both arms and swung her around. "I want you to know you've bewitched me, woman! You make me feel like a ten-year-old again. You make me want to stand on the tops of tall buildings and beat my chest, and jump out of haylofts, and do cartwheels down Coronado Freeway at rush hour!" Cassidy gave a sputter of laughter and Logan grinned, suddenly boyish. "What I'm trying to say, Cass, is that I think I—" The harsh bray of a horn interrupted him rudely. There was a war whoop behind them, the snarl of a straining engine, yells and shouts of laughter. Logan stared over her head, then slowly let her slide to the ground. "Well, hell," he sighed in resignation. "I think they've found us, Cass."

Cassidy turned around. A dilapidated red pickup truck came rocketing toward them, sand spraying as the driver gunned the engine and the truck fishtailed up the last slope. A tall, sunburned figure was riding shotgun, standing up half out of the truck cab and hanging onto the open doorframe. The truck shot into the air, and he gave another rebel yell, riding the truck like a rodeo rider mastering a bronco. Another figure was standing in the box, legs widespread, hands gripping the black rollbar curving over the cab. All of them were grinning like bandits, obviously relishing the wild ride.

The driver brought the truck into a tight U-turn beside the folded balloon, spraying dust and stones. The two passengers vaulted out before it had even rocked to a stop, and Logan raised his clenched fist in a sign of victory, grinning broadly as they strode toward him.

"Damned near lost you, boy!" The older man shoved his Stetson onto the back of his head and gave Logan a brotherly slap on the back.

"Thought we'd seen the last of you, Logan!" shouted the second man, doing a fast little two-step as he neared, fists raised. "Where the hell were you headed? Mexico?"

"Lose your compass?" The third figure jumped out of the truck. It was a woman, small and lithe and sunbronzed, her features holding a hint of her Indian heritage. She had tucked her jet black hair into a battered Stetson and tendrils had worked free, blowing across her cheeks. She brushed them back impatiently, giving Cassidy a speculative glance. "Or just get a little distracted?"

Logan responded to their good-natured teasing with a laugh. "Navigation trouble," he explained, giving Cassidy a quick, private smile over their heads. "And you could have taken a bit more time getting here."

The woman gave a snort, striding over to Cassidy and staring at her boldly. "I'm Rona Estavez O'Brien," she said, thrusting out her hand. "The tall one's my husband, Derek, and the kid's Jeff Chapman." Her sunbrowned fingers folded around Cassidy's firmly. "You do good work, Yorke. Your dinner hour show's too damned cute for words, but you've got good potential. Dump the zoo circuit and featherweight interviews, and you'd have one hell of a program there."

Cassidy stared at her in astonishment, then started to laugh. "My sentiments exactly! How about giving my exec producer a call?"

"Maybe I'll do just that," Rona replied with a decisive nod. "And if that doesn't work, we'll overthrow the damn place and produce our own show."

"God help Albuquerque," muttered Derek from behind them. "That's all we need—a renegade news reporter and a quarter-blood Apache civil rights' activist staging a coup at the local TV station!"

The five of them laughed together, then set to work dismantling the burner frame and fuel tanks and packing the balloon in its protective bag. Logan and his crew were a smooth team, each knowing exactly what to do, no one getting in anyone else's way. They seemed to accept Cassidy unquestioningly, pleased when she offered to help, patiently showing her what to do, including her in their teasing until she felt like she'd known the four of them for years.

"Come on, you guys, speed it up!" Jeff urged with an impatient glance at his watch. "The fund-raising banquet's going to start in a couple of hours. If we time it right, we can miss the speeches and rubber chicken and get there in time for the champagne and dancing."

"Which reminds me," Logan put in, rummaging around in a wooden locker mounted in the truck bed. "Where's that—here it is." He straightened, holding up a bottle of champagne. He vaulted down lightly, peeling the wire cage off the bottle and working the cork loose with his thumbs.

It gave with a loud pop and sprayed foaming champagne over Cassidy.

"Logan!" Laughing, she licked the sweetness from her lips. "What is this—baptism by champagne?"

"More or less." He filled the five styrofoam cups that Rona had produced. They each took a cup and Logan reached across to touch the rim of his to Cassidy's. "To dreams coming true, flygirl."

"Thank you, Logan," she whispered, knowing that he wasn't talking about her first balloon ride at all. She felt light-headed, and wondered if it was the exhilaration of her first balloon flight, the altitude, or those laughing indigo eyes locked with hers that was making her so giddy.

Then the others crowded around with laughter and congratulations, Derek and Jeff both honoring her with a ritual hug and kiss. Someone refilled her cup and she sipped the champagne happily. It was warm and starting to go flat, but she couldn't remember ever tasting anything so delicious. Logan's gaze caught hers again and she smiled, feeling her pulse leap as that warmly intimate glance held hers meaningfully. *I love you!* she very nearly shouted then and there, feeling as though she could dance back to Albuquerque without once touching solid ground. My God, was it really possible? she mused. Did love really strike like this, shooting out of a cloudless sky like a lightning bolt?

"More?"

Cassidy blinked, realizing that Jeff was standing beside her with the champagne bottle poised over her cup. "Good grief, no! Any more and I'll be able to fly back to town without ever unpacking that balloon."

"Miss Yorke has a low tolerance for alchohol," Logan put in lazily, taking the cup from her hand and setting it aside. "One sip too many, and she becomes completely unmanageable."

"I seem to remember you managing quite well the other night," she murmured, slipping him a glance underneath her lashes as they strolled toward the truck.

"I'd like to manage you into my bed right now," he shot back in a husky growl. "And then I'd like to manage the most unbelievable things you've ever—"

"Hey, you two, pick it up!" Rona shouted from the cab of the truck. "We've got a long drive back."

Although Cassidy wouldn't have believed it possible, the five of them managed to cram themselves into the cab of the truck and still leave Rona room to drive. After much elbowing and cheerful complaining, they finally got under way. Cassidy found herself wedged comfortably in Logan's lap, his strong arms holding her tightly against him as Rona muscled the truck back to the highway.

"The balloon ride's the easy part," Jeff told her dryly. "It's Rona's driving that'll kill ya!"

Cassidy laughed at Rona's prompt suggestion that he could get out and walk anytime he wanted to. They settled into a rollicking banter that was obviously part of a friendly, long-standing feud, and Cassidy nestled against Logan comfortably, utterly happy.

It took over an hour to get back to the launch site in spite of Rona's breakneck driving. They were among the first back. The rally site looked more like an abandoned Gypsy encampment than ever, with a few trucks and cars parked here and there and people sprawled around waiting patiently. The only balloonists returning this early were those who, like Cassidy and Logan, had drifted off-course and had given up or had run into mechanical trouble. One by one they straggled in, trucks and ancient station wagons burdened with balloons and equipment. They were greeted with catcalls and whistles and good-natured jeers as they returned in defeat, looking dusty and happily exhausted.

None of them seemed particularly disappointed at not having finished the race. The two teams that had suffered mechanical trouble were promptly surrounded by people offering knowledgeable help, tools and repair kits appearing like magic. Someone handed Cassidy a still-simmering hot dog and she attacked it ravenously, helping herself to a sip from the bottle of ice-cold beer that she was sharing with Logan. More and more people were coming in now. They milled around, hot dogs and beer in hand, laughing and joking as they greeted friends they hadn't seen since the last rally, or trading technical advice with strangers.

Logan and Derek stowed some last bits of gear in the back of the truck, then strolled back to join Cassidy and Rona. "What are we doing now?" Derek asked around a mouthful of the hot dog he'd taken from Rona's hand. "It'll be hours before everyone gets in. There's a party here later. Want to hang around for that, or head back to town for the banquet?"

"Logan's one of the celebrity guests at the fund-raising banquet tonight, you idiot," Rona reminded her husband as she retrieved her half-eaten hot dog. "And Cassidy is too. They don't have any choice about the banquet."

"That reminds me," Derek put in. "Your station won the race, Cass. Word just came in a few minutes ago."

"Really!" Cassidy laughed in delight, glancing at Logan. "My boss is going to be a little upset that I wasn't there to give a blow-by-blow of the win, Mr. Wilde."

"Tell him to sue me," Logan drawled, leaning over and taking a bite out of her hot dog. "And if we're going to make that banquet, we should start back to town about now." He finished the beer in one long swallow and slipped his arm around her waist, herding her gently through the crowd. "You didn't really want to wait for McGuire and dePaul, did you?"

"I should. They'll want some footage for tonight's eleven o'clock news. It's going to look a little odd, KALB winning the race and their celebrity guest not even here to congratulate them. Especially," she added with a grin, "when I was supposed to be in that balloon!"

They strolled toward Logan's Ferrari. "Do you want to stay?" he asked quite seriously.

She gave him a sidelong look. "Not really."

Smiling, Logan pulled the car door open for her and Cassidy slid into the low leather seat, wondering idly what Ken Vaughn and Milt Cordova were going to say about her disappearance. Not, she decided with a smile, that she particularly cared. Although if she'd thought her date with Logan had led to some interesting speculation, today's little adventure should really stir things up.

"What are you smiling about?"

Cassidy laughed softly. "You. Me. This entire evening. God knows what rumors are already going around about us. Ken will be losing his mind. Here's the perfect follow-up to my interview with you, and he can't even find me!"

"Do you want to call him and tell him all about it?" he murmured. He leaned toward her and drew her gently toward him.

"Not in the least." Cassidy kissed him lightly. "At this moment, I don't care if I ever talk to Ken Vaughn again or not."

"Good." He ran his lips across her cheek. "You didn't really want to go to that banquet, did you?"

Cassidy's heart skipped a beat. She let her head fall back as his mouth explored the angle of her jaw. "What did you have in mind?"

"Dinner. With me. Alone. Steaks and good wine. Brandy in front of a crackling fire."

She swallowed, knowing that if she said yes she was agreeing to considerably more than just steak and brandy. And yet, she mused, was there ever really any question? "I don't think they'll miss me," she whispered. "KALB's going to be well represented. But what about you? Won't they miss you at the head table?"

Logan kissed her softly, then straightened and started the engine. "The only banquet I want tonight is you."

It was dusk by the time they cruised to a stop in front of Logan's apartment building. The valet had Cassidy's door open before Logan had even turned off the engine, and she glanced around at Logan with a smile as she started to step out.

He was staring out the windshield, frowning, his profile pensive and hard against the glowing copper sky. He made no effort to get out of the car and after a moment Cassidy sank back into the contoured seat uncertainly. He had been quiet and thoughtful ever since they had reached the city limits, and Cassidy had decided that he had been thinking about the rally. But suddenly she had a sinking feeling that it wasn't that simple.

Tentatively, she put her hand on his arm. "Logan, if you're having second thoughts about tonight—"

"Not about you," he interrupted flatly, his eyes hard and angry as he stared out at the tall building. "It's this—place." He spat the word like poison. Then, abruptly, not even looking at her, he started the car again. "Shut that door."

"But I..." She stared at him in bewilderment. Not knowing what else to do, she pulled the car door closed.

"Not here," he suddenly said. "I don't want to make love to you here tonight, surrounded by lies. You're not part of this life, part of this...me." He looked at her, his eyes smoky and warm. "Tonight's too special for that," he said with a husky promise in his voice that made her breath catch. "Tonight's just for you and me, Cass. And Logan Wilde doesn't have a damned thing to do with it."

"I—I don't understand," she whispered in confusion.

"I know." He slammed the car into gear and floored the accelerator. The Ferrari screamed past the astonished valet, tires smoking. "They may own me, body and soul, but my heart's still mine to give to whomever I damned well choose—at least they can't take *that* from me!"

Eight

The Ferrari shot onto the street, snarling and fishtailing like a startled cat on linoleum. Cassidy glanced nervously at the steadily rising needle on the speedometer. Logan was staring out the windshield, jaw set, eyes narrowed as he zigzagged in and out of traffic. A black Firebird veered in front of them, two teenaged boys grinning through the rear window. Logan swore, braking sharply, and Cassidy grabbed the dashboard with a gasp.

Logan glanced at her. Then, almost sheepishly, he eased back on the accelerator until they reached the speed limit. "Sorry," he muttered after a moment. "Pretty childish."

"Let's say you weren't exactly setting a good example for those kids in the Firebird," she breathed, unknotting her fingers from the dashboard. "And I have a hungry little mouth at home depending on my safe return."

Logan gave her a startled glance. "A *what?*"

"Cat," she reassured him with a dry smile. "Samantha Tarbottom Yorke, to be specific. She's been my best friend for nearly fifteen years, and she'd be pretty upset if you were the cause of my untimely demise. As clever as she is, she can't quite manage that can opener on her own. No thumbs."

Logan laughed. "And what would Samantha have to say if you didn't get home tonight?"

She gave him a look of sublime innocence. "Is there a chance of that?"

"If I have anything to say about it."

She smiled. "She won't go hungry—I'll call my neighbor and ask her to feed her—but she'll give me the cold shoulder treatment when I finally do get home."

"And what if you were gone for the entire weekend?"

Cassidy's heart gave a thump. "She may never talk to me again."

He reached across and gave her fingers a squeeze. "I'm pretty good with old maid cats—a bowl of cream, a tin of salmon, a scratch behind the ears, and I have them eating out of my hand." He suddenly laughed. "Why Tarbottom?"

"My father. When Sam was a kitten, she walked across a newly tarred stretch of road near our house and got covered with the stuff. I don't know what upset Dad more—the fact that the vet charged twenty dollars to clean her up, or that she'd gotten out of the yard and onto the street. He'd never admit it, but he loves her as much as I do. Mom says he keeps two pictures on his nighttable—one of me, and one of Sam. And he sends us *both* birthday presents!"

"Sounds like quite a family you left behind."

Cassidy nodded, smiling fondly. "They are. Those brothers of mine drove me crazy for years, and now I sometimes miss them all so badly that for two cents I'd toss Sam and my toothbrush into a suitcase and go back. Then I remember I'm supposed to be a big girl now, and I phone instead." She looked at Logan. "And you? Do your parents live in Albuquerque?"

"My parents are dead."

He said it so matter-of-factly, so calmly, that it took Cassidy a moment to realize what he meant. "Oh, Logan—!"

"Car accident," he said just as calmly, watching the traffic. "Two and a half years ago. They were coming back from a vacation in Mexico. A pickup full of illegal aliens running the border at night, lights off, ran into them. Mom, Dad, two Mexican women and a baby were killed. My sister, Jacqueline, is still in a coma. She's been in the Hutcheson clinic for the past two years. It's one of the few facilities set up to care for that type of thing."

"Oh, my God," Cassidy whispered. "Logan, I—I don't even know what to say. I'm so sorry."

"I keep telling myself it could have been worse." He took a deep breath. "I could have lost Jackie, too."

"Are you sure you don't want to attend the fund-raising banquet tonight?" she asked quietly. "It must mean a lot to you—the Hutcheson, I mean."

Logan's smile was bitter. "It does," he said roughly. "But I'd rather spend the evening with you than at a banquet trying to pretend that—" He gave his head a shake and lapsed into brooding silence.

Cassidy put her hand out and he caught it and braided his fingers with hers, resting it on his thigh. She gave his hand an understanding squeeze and relaxed back into the lush leather seat, sensing that what he needed just now was silent companionship, not all the puzzled questions whirling around in her mind. There had been absolutely nothing in any of the media hype surrounding the Hutcheson fund-raising about Logan's personal interest in the facility. And although she could understand him not wanting to make a huge issue out of something so painful, the blunt truth was that it would help bring in money. And why had none of the press kit profiles mentioned a sister? Perhaps the Hutcheson wanted it that way, she decided; perhaps they thought the publicity associated with someone of Logan's notoriety didn't fit their sedate and serious image.

She was so lost in thought that she didn't even notice that Logan had turned off the highway until the Ferrari rocked to a stop and Logan got out. She blinked and sat up, looking around in surprise. They were in the mountains. Dark tree-fringed crags scalloped the sky and she took a deep breath of the tart, bitter scent of pine pitch. It was nearly dark now, and she could barely make out Logan's form on the road ahead. He was unlatching a high wooden gate and as he walked it open, Cassidy lifted herself over the gearshift console. She drove the car through the gate, then put it in neutral and slid back into the passenger seat as Logan relatched the gate and walked back to the car.

He gave her a grin of thanks as he pulled the car door closed. "I thought you were asleep."

"Just thinking. Where are we?"

"You'll see." He smiled mysteriously.

Cassidy swallowed her curiosity with an effort, staring out into the darkness with renewed interest. The road wound along the floor of a valley, trees and rock looming above them on either side. It was wild and desolate and incredibly peaceful, and even the Ferrari seemed subdued as it glided along the narrow road, the purr of the engine all but lost under the sound of wind in high pines. They started to climb. The turns became sharper and more frequent as the road zigzagged up the mountainside. Every now and again the trees would thin and Cassidy would get a tantalizing glimpse of starlit plains far below. Finally it leveled out, and Cassidy caught her breath. They were high up, very high up, and spread out below them was a vast panoramic view of what looked like the entire state. A patch of twinkling lights far below them caught Cassidy's eye, and she gave an exclamation of surprise as she realized it was Albuquerque.

"It's like being in heaven!" she said with a delighted laugh.

"Closest you'll ever come and still be on earth."

The road turned abruptly to the right. Logan swung the car into the velvet darkness beneath a stand of towering pines. He stopped the car and cut the engine, and in the sudden silence Cassidy could hear a dog's excited barking. She looked expectantly at Logan but he was already swinging out of the car, and after a moment's puzzled contemplation she did the same thing. The night air was fresh and cold and spiced faintly with wood smoke. Above them, the lush pines moaned and whispered in the breeze, their moon-flecked trunks creaking gently. As her eyes adapted to the darkness, she saw the cabin. It was set well back in the pines, sheltered and inviting.

"Hey—Buster!" The sound of paws pattered swiftly through the darkness and a huge shadow launched itself at Logan. Laughing, he wrestled with the delighted dog for a moment, then spoke sharply to it. It stopped its play instantly and stood quivering with excitement.

"Hi." Cassidy held her hand out. "Buster?"

Hearing his name, the dog bounded delightedly toward her. It shoved its big face into her hand and snuffled her fingers. A warm pink tongue laved her palm as a sign of his approval, and he stared adoringly up at her as she scratched his jowls and ears.

"Now you've done it," Logan warned her. "He'll be under your feet at every step now, crawling into your lap whenever he thinks you're not looking. Not only is he the world's poorest excuse for a watchdog, but he's also the biggest baby ever born."

As if to disprove his words, Buster suddenly whirled around, ears cocked, and gave a couple of self-important barks. A cat appeared from out of the shadows and trotted toward them. Buster gave another bark but the cat simply ran between his legs as though he wasn't even there and wrapped itself around Logan's ankles, then Cassidy's, purring like a buzz saw.

"Come on." Logan reached for her hand, laughing. "I guess it's safe to take you in now the welcoming committee's given its approval."

When Logan unlocked the cabin door and turned on a light, Cassidy's first realization was that this was no hermit's retreat, but a comfortable home. It was much larger than she had thought. A huge sunken living room filled with overstuffed sofas and big chairs ran the entire front of the cabin. The cathedral ceiling sloped to a full two stories at the outside wall, which was totally glass. The view would be spectacular, she knew, a panorama of pines and the New Mexican landscape. There was a second floor gallery overlooking the living room, off which ran doors that Cassidy supposed led to the bedrooms.

The living room had been beautifully decorated. The pine walls and floors had been left their natural color and the pale golden wood was highlighted by woven Indian rugs and pottery. A stone fireplace dominated one entire end of the room and Cassidy walked toward it slowly, entranced by the entire room, the entire cabin. Books were everywhere, filling the bookcases flanking the fireplace, and overflowing from shelves and low tables. Near the fireplace, turned so it faced the windows, sat a massive oak desk. It, too, was covered with books and papers and magazines, and an obviously well used electric typewriter sat dead center.

"This is gorgeous!" Cassidy looked around in delight. Logan was still standing near the door, one hip leaned against the carved wooden railing overlooking the living room. "Who does it belong to?"

"Joel Logan."

"Logan?" She strolled toward the windows, seeing nothing but reflections of the room behind her. "Relative?"

"Close." He gave a quiet laugh and walked down the two steps into the living room. "I'm Joel Logan."

Cassidy turned to look at him, mouth already curving in a smile. Then she saw his expression and her smile faded away. "You're what?"

"I'm Joel Logan," he repeated quietly. "And this is my home."

"But..." Cassidy stared at him. "But you can't be," she said in a reasonable tone. After all, she'd seen Logan Wilde's press kit photograph, and this was the same man. "I mean, I interviewed Logan Wilde. I mean, I interviewed you." She took a deep breath and tried again. "If you're Joel Logan, then who on earth is Logan Wilde?"

"I have no idea," he said quietly.

"But—" She gestured vaguely, totally bewildered. "But you're living in his apartment."

"Logan Wilde doesn't exist, Cass. He's an invention. Someone my publisher needs to sell books; someone the magazines need to sell more copies. He's just a byline."

Cassidy stared at him in disbelief. "But—but the apartment, the whirlpool, the car..."

"Props. Paid for by my publisher." He smiled that same bitter smile she'd seen before. "After all, I have an image to keep up. It's just a high priced motel room, Cass. There's not a damned thing up there that's mine. It's just a...prop."

"And the books?" she asked faintly.

"Mine." He smiled wearily. "I really am a writer, Cass."

Some of the astonishment was finally wearing off. "But...why?"

"Money." He sighed again and walked across to the fireplace. He moved the screen aside and lit a match to the kindling. "I was always able to make a decent living writing adventure novels, mysteries, westerns, whatever. They weren't making me rich, but I never wanted for anything. Then after the accident, I realized I'd have to do better if I was going to give Jackie the care she needs. Dad left me this place—the house and land—and I thought for a while I was going to have to sell it. But I couldn't do it." He gave a dry laugh. "This damned house is the only family I've got besides Jackie. So I had to come up with something else. For kicks, I approached *Playboy* about writing a bachelor's advice column. They liked the idea, although the first thing they did was change my name to Logan Wilde—said it sounded more macho or some damned thing. The column caught on and was syndicated. Then a while later I jokingly said something to my agent and publisher about a Logan Wilde book." He gave a snort of laughter, adding a stick of kindling to the growing flame. "The rest is history. At first it was fun. I was making the money I needed, I enjoyed the talk shows and publicity tours, the parties, the women." He stared into the flames, silent. "Then I discovered I'd created a monster. Logan Wilde started taking over my entire life. The more popular he became, the worse it got. Sometimes I sit in that penthouse apartment and wonder if Joel Logan ever really existed at all, or if he's the invention, and Logan Wilde the reality."

"Can't you quit?" Cassidy asked quietly, coming over to stand beside him. "Can't you bump Logan Wilde off or something?"

He looked up at her, mouth twitching in a humorless smile. "Contracts, honey. I'm signed up for at least another three books. And a clause in those contracts forbids me to reveal who Logan Wilde really is. A handful of people around here know, of course. Jeff, Derek and Rona, a few friends of Mom and Dad's, Katherine Salazar and a few others at the Hutcheson. You." His smile took on real warmth for a moment, then faded away altogether. "But if word ever gets out that Logan Wilde doesn't exist—that he's really just a local country boy who used to write cowboy stories for a living—I'd wind up in a lawsuit for breach of contract. And, frankly, Wilde makes more money than Joel does, money I need. Money I've already spent on medication, doctors, lab work, specialists."

"But if you hate it so much," Cassidy persisted, "why play their games? You could write the books without playing the rest of the role. You're selling out!"

"Don't lecture me on selling out, Cassidy!" he said with quiet intensity, standing up abruptly. "That gorgeous, sexy woman flirting her way through the news twice a day on KALB is no more the real Cassidy Yorke than I'm the real Logan Wilde. So don't get self-righteous with me, damn it!"

A hot blush poured across Cassidy's cheeks. She turned away, shoulders stiff, and Logan swore softly. "Honey, I'm sorry."

"Don't apologize." Cassidy took a deep breath. "It's true. I *am* selling out. And I hate it as much as you hate playing Logan Wilde." Suddenly, in spite of Logan's anger and her own embarrassed indignation, she started to laugh. "My God, what a pair of frauds we are! Between the two of us, we've got more personalities than a Hitchcock movie."

Logan—Joel—laughed, suddenly relaxing. He slipped his arms around her and hugged her fiercely. "What did I ever do before I met you? You've brought something bright back into my life, Cass Yorke. It's been hell these past two years, living a lie, afraid to get close to anyone because I couldn't afford the risk of being found out. You can't imagine how good it feels to let go of the games and masks and just be me for a while." He kissed her gently. "And sharing it with you makes it that much better. That was the worst part the other night—knowing you mistrusted Logan Wilde, wanting to tell you the truth but not trusting you enough. Hating myself for not trusting you."

"Oh, Lo—Joel, I mean!" She smiled. "This could get complicated, trying to remember which man I'm with—Logan Wilde in public, and Joel Logan in private. Every time I'm with one of you I'll feel like I'm two-timing the other one."

He laughed and pulled the fireplace screen closed. "Joel's the good-looking one you're sleeping with," he teased. "That's all you have to remember."

"It all sounds deliciously wicked," Cassidy said with a smile as she wandered along the bookcase, perusing the titles. "I never thought I'd—" A familiar title caught her eye and she reached for it, eyes widening when it finally hit her. "My God!" She wheeled toward Joel excitedly. "You're Hackamore Hayes! I mean, you're the J.J. Logan who writes the Hackamore Hayes books!" She gave a delighted laugh. "My dad's got every Hackamore Hayes novel ever written. And that secret agent series about—oh, what's his name! The guy who teaches medieval poetry at Princeton between government jobs—"

"Dexter Kincaid."

"That's it! Dexter 'Dangerman' Kincaid!" She gave another laugh of sheer delight. "Oh, Joel, wait until I tell dad that I—" She stopped abruptly, her excitement evaporating. "Well, damn," she muttered sourly. "I can't tell him, can I?"

Joel smiled sympathetically, taking the book from her hand. "I don't know why not, as long as you don't go into any details. Here, I'll sign this copy for him."

Cassidy's gloom vanished. "Oh, would you? He'll go absolutely out of his mind when he sees it."

"Anything for the father of the most important woman in my life," he told her with a grin. "What's your dad's name?"

"James." Joel signed the book with a flourish and handed it back to her. Cassidy looked at the signature and smiled, then set the book aside. She slipped her arms around Joel's neck, running her fingers through his thick, curly hair. "Thank you, J.J. Logan. No wonder I couldn't figure you out. I couldn't understand why I kept seeing two different men every time I was with you, why I kept responding to Logan when ordinarily I detest that type of cool operator. But it wasn't Logan I was responding to at all. It was you." She laughed delightedly. "One minute I'd want to slap that smug Logan Wilde smile off your face, the next I'd want to—"

"You'd want to what?" he urged softly.

"Oh...things." She frowned very slightly, toying with his top shirt button. "Were you going to feed your little zoo? They seem to be watching us anxiously."

"The man who takes care of this place when I'm away lives in a cabin just up the road. He keeps everyone very well fed. Now to get back to what you were saying..."

"Joel—" She stepped out of his embrace and walked across to the fireplace. "What about the women in Logan Wilde's life?" She hadn't really wanted to ask it, but the words seemed to pop out of their own accord. She ran her finger along the carved mantle, not looking at him. "Were they just . . . props, too?"

She heard him sigh. "Cass . . ." His footsteps neared and a moment later his hands settled on her shoulders. "Honey, you're probably not going to believe this, but all those stories in my books about my sexual exploits are just that—stories. Fantasies designed to give Logan Wilde the credibility he needs to sell the books." He laughed softly. "Logan Wilde is every man's erotic dream come true, Cass."

Cassidy turned to look up at him. "So you haven't really done all the things you write about?"

Joel laughed again. "Honey, I couldn't possibly make love to all those women and still have time to write the books and make the public appearances." He combed her hair back with his fingers and cupped her head. "The women are real enough. They're part of the job, just like the talk show circuit, the book tours. They're part of the image. I'm expected to escort last week's beauty pageant winner to this charitable event, this week's starlet to that celebrity's party. I pose for the pictures and say witty things for the reporters, and then I escort the lady home. Then usually," he added with a hint of humor, "I go home and sleep alone."

"Usually." Again, it slipped out unplanned.

"I'm only human, Cass," he reminded her dryly. "Once in a while—once in a very long while—I'll take what's offered." He kissed the side of her throat. "Cass, I could count the number of women who've shared that bed with me on the fingers of one hand. And—though God knows I'm not very proud of this—they leave in the morning, and I never see them again."

To her surpise, Cassidy discovered she believed him. "An admission like that could ruin you," she teased.

"Tell anyone, and I'll deny it flatly," he murmured with a chuckle. "Even Joel Logan has his pride." He tugged her against him. "Now, a few minutes ago you started telling me about 'things.' Just what sort of 'things' did you have in mind?"

Cassidy shrugged, running her fingernail down the placket of his shirt. "Well," she murmured as she slipped the top button free, "I could tell you. Or—" the next button slipped open "—I could show you."

Joel's breathing caught slightly as she slipped one button after another free with deliberate slowness. She glanced up at him through her lashes. "Would you like that?"

"Oh, yes!" He caught his breath as she slowly ran her fingernail down his chest and stomach. "I'd like that a whole lot."

Nine

Smiling mischievously, Cassidy backed away from him, sliding the zipper on the front of her playsuit slowly downward. Joel went motionless, entranced as it moved ever downward, baring her to him. Enjoying teasing him, she slipped out of the suit and let it fall to her hips. She reached behind her and unhooked her lacy bra, then slowly let the straps slide off her shoulders.

"Oh, God, Cass," Joel groaned, eyes fastened on her hungrily as she let the bra drop. "You're so beautiful!" He stepped toward her and Cassidy put her hands inside his open shirt and ran them up to rest lightly on his shoulders. He covered one small, firm breast with his hand, his eyes burning into hers as he stroked the hardening peak with his open palm. It was deliciously rough against the sensitive nipple and Cassidy shivered slightly. His fingers parted, closed again with the nipple between them, and he squeezed it with rhythmic gentleness.

Little electric shocks darted through her and Cassidy's eyes slid closed. "Oh, Joel..."

His mouth covered hers, warm and ready, his tongue seeking hers urgently. Cassidy moaned softly and pressed her breast more firmly into his hand, opening her mouth fully to him in instinctive and trusting surrender. Her breath caught slightly as his other hand ran down the satiny skin on her stomach. Then he fumbled with the zipper of his jeans. It parted smoothly and Joel took one of her hands and guided it gently downward.

He was vitally, urgently ready for her and he groaned softly as she caressed him. Emboldened by his uninhibited pleasure, she tugged the top of his jeans down and pressed herself against him, loving the feel of him against her bare stomach. He ran his hands down her back and under the playsuit and flimsy panties. He slid them over her hips, catching his breath when she gave a helpful wriggle to free herself of the confining fabric.

"Joel!" Panting, she tried to fit herself over him, driven half-wild by his tantalizing touch.

"Wait, darling," he groaned, skinning out of his jeans and briefs. "I don't want the mood broken by a close encounter of any kind with that zipper!" Then he slipped the shirt off and flung it aside. "Now," he growled, "where were we?" He caught her against him roughly, moving his hips in an evocative rhythm that nearly made Cassidy faint. She clutched him closer, feeling the muscles in his back ripple under the damp, smooth skin as she moved her own hips in counterpoint.

"Now," she moaned softly, wrapping her arms around his neck. "Oh, Joel, I want you so much!"

He murmured something, caressing her back in long, urgent strokes, cupping his hands around her bottom and lifting her against him. "I'm yours, Cassie—completely." His mouth moved hungrily on hers as he drew her leg up over his hip. "Show me what you want. Tell me how—oh...God! Cassidy!" He gave an astonished gasp as, in one lithe, deft movement she wrapped both legs around his thighs and brought him inside her. His fingers sank into her bottom as he supported her, his teeth bared in exquisite agony as he tried to catch his breath.

Cassidy gave a little gasp of satisfaction and arched her back to make it even more complete. Letting her head fall back, eyes closed, she moved slowly against him to take him into her as deeply as possible.

Legs braced, Joel gripped her hips firmly, guiding her, and she let him set the pace. "I've got so much to learn," she whispered against his ear, tightening her thighs on his and undulating her hips in a slow, silken circle that made Joel groan. She scraped her teeth gentle across his earlobe, feeling his breath catch. "Teach me, Joel. Show me what's best for you."

"What's best for me is knowing I'm pleasing you," he moaned, his mouth hot and damp on her shoulder, her throat. "I love hearing that little catch in your breath when I do this . . . or this. I love the feel of you around me."

"Oh, Joel!" She gave an urgent wriggle as the hot, melting tension within her sharpened, suddenly unable to be close enough, to move as freely or as fully as instinct dictated.

"Hang on, darling," Joel growled, responding to the need in her voice and movements. He knelt slowly, still holding her against him.

Sitting in his lap, she smiled and kissed him, running her fingers through his damp, tangled hair. "Afraid of heights, Mr. Logan?"

"Afraid of dropping you at an inconvenient moment," he murmured in reply, kissing her throat and shoulder as he cradled her in one arm and used the other for balance as he slowly tipped her backward.

Cassidy sighed comfortably as he laid her gently back on the braided rug, still cradled intimately between her thighs. She stretched her cramped legs, smiling. "A little less adventurous, but much, much better."

"Anything to please you," he murmured, starting to move with slow, strong intensity. He was watching her, eyes heavy lidded and sultry. "Anything at all."

"Oh, Joel..." Cassidy's breath caught as his body coaxed the most incredible sensations from hers. That exquisite heavy warmth was starting to build with increasing urgency, setting her body atingle as it swelled in ever-higher waves. She groaned softly, closing her eyes and moving under him with growing abandon, and his own movements became stronger in response to her need. Each silken movement of his hips brought her ever nearer until she was sobbing with it, clutching at his shoulders and gasping his name over and over. He was whispering something now, coaxing her on, adjusting his every move to satisfy her, to bring her to that final, breathless pinnacle.

"Joel!" It burst through her, white-hot, a splintering, shivering explosion that went on and on until she cried out, arching blindly toward him. Vaguely, like an echo, she heard another voice lifted with hers, and was vaguely aware of Joel's hands locked around her hips as he gasped and gave one final, urgent thrust. He strained against her, his hands pulling her fiercely against him.

Like aftershocks following a major quake, tingles of that final ecstasy washed through Cassidy in wave after ebbing wave. She panted for breath, feeling rivulets of perspiration trickling down Joel's cheek where it was pressed against hers. She closed her eyes, the taut muscles in her legs and arms slowly relaxing. "Oh, Joel," she whispered in exhausted wonder. "I never dreamed it could be like this."

He stirred, taking a deep breath. "Neither did I, Cass," he whispered.

She opened her eyes and found him staring down at her. He smiled and kissed her gently, in that special way of lovers. "It doesn't seem possible," she murmured, caressing his mouth with her fingertips. "I didn't know falling in love could happen like this, so fast, so certain, so... right."

"What did you say?" He turned his head to kiss her palm. "Say that again."

She smiled, not even surprised to realize that she had said it aloud, and even less surprised to realize that it was true. "I said I love you. I don't know how or why, but I think I fell in love with you—Joel Logan, not Logan Wilde—about ten minutes after you walked into the KALB studios." She gave a shy laugh, blushing suddenly. "You probably don't want to hear this. You probably have a dozen women a day falling in love with you."

"With Logan Wilde, not Joel Logan," he corrected gently. "And it's Joel who's in love with you."

"Really?" She touched his face wonderingly. "You're not just . . . just saying it because I did?"

He laughed quietly. "I said I love you, Cassidy Yorke. I'll carve it into every tree trunk on the place if you want me to—'Joel Logan loves Cassidy Yorke.'"

"With a heart around it?"

"Of course."

"I've never been in love before."

"Never?"

"Well . . ." She frowned thoughtfully. "Once, I guess. If you count Elliot Masterson in the third grade. It didn't last, though. Kevin caught him trying to kiss me after school one day and beat the daylights out of him. After that, poor Elliot wouldn't even look at me."

Joel groaned. "Great! I fall in love with a beautiful, sexy woman only to discover she's got three brothers who make a hobby out of pulverizing her suitors."

Cassidy laughed. "Believe me, it was no joke for me, either! My two youngest brothers were both on the football team when I was in high school. Some poor guy would come up to me in the hallway just to talk, and two minutes later he'd turn pale and bolt. I'd turn around and there'd be Chris or Steve. They'd just be standing there, smiling. And flexing their muscles."

"They're not coming out to New Mexico in the foreseeable future, are they?"

"No. Kevin's married now, and Chris is in college. Steve's at home helping dad in the store; dad keeps him too busy to visit."

"I thought your dad was a farmer."

"Nope. Dad has a hardware store in town. But we live on my granddad's farm, and mom raises ducks, a few chickens, a goose or two. One of my uncles actually farms the land."

He smiled, stroking her cheekbones with his thumbs. "It sure—hey!" He recoiled like he'd been shot.

"Joel, what on earth . . . ?"

"This damned dog!" Joel reached around and hauled Buster into view by the scruff of his neck. "He's got a nose like a block of ice!"

Cassidy went into gales of laughter, patting Joel's left buttock soothingly. Buster's nose print was still there, damp and cold. "I think he's suggesting we stop this shameless cavorting and feed him."

"He's already—oh, I give up." He turned his head away as a purring black cat pushed between them. He eased himself free of Cassidy and sat beside her, wincing when the cat tried to crawl into his lap.

Cassidy sat up and scooped the cat into her arms. "Watch the claws, darling," she murmured into a feline ear. "That's the man I love that you're threatening with grievous injury."

"Damned grievous!" Joel said with feeling. "I suppose if I'm going to get any peace, I'd better feed the entire crew."

"Me, too!" Cassidy put in firmly. "You promised me steak and wine, remember?"

"Steak and wine, it is. Then," he added with a promising grin that made Cassidy's heart leap, "I'm banishing the four-footed ones to the great outdoors so I can make love to my woman without an advisory committee standing by."

Cassidy awoke slowly, drifting toward the new day with a feeling of the most utter contentment she had ever known. She was still lying tucked into the curve of Joel's body, spoon-fashion with his long body pressed tightly against her back, his arms cradling her lovingly. His breath was warm and moist on the back of her neck and she smiled drowsily into the pillow. Sound asleep! And rightfully so, she mused. After last night's shameless excesses, the poor man would probably sleep into the middle of next week!

Her smile widened. They hadn't been able to keep their hands off each other last night. They'd been like children turned loose in a candy store, unable to get their fill of each other, greedy for every caress and touch and taste. The entire night was a delicious blur of seemingly endless lovemaking now, although she sleepily remembered that they had gotten up once and had shared a leisurely shower. They'd soaped each other with slow, wondrous care, touching and kissing until their bodies had again responded to the magic of each other. They had tumbled out, wet and slippery and laughing, and had made love right there on the thick bath mat.

Even thinking about it made her feel weak and warm. The sensation of Joel's naked body pressed against her back made her tingle and she leaned back against him, her breath catching very slightly. Joel stirred. His hand closed gently on her breast and he nuzzled her hair aside to kiss the nape of her neck lingeringly. Cassidy murmured in wordless pleasure, giving a little intake of breath when Joel circled the betraying hardness of her nipple with the tip of his finger. He rubbed his finger across the sensitive bud again and again until Cassidy moaned his name softly and laid her head back against his chest. She reached back and ran a caressing hand down his hip and thigh, feeling the unmistakable evidence of his own arousal stir against her.

He ran his flattened palm down over the slight feminine swell of her stomach, then lower. Cassidy held her breath, giving a convulsive little shiver as he caressed her delicately. He stroked her lightly, knowledgeably, and Cassidy let her eyes slide closed as she murmured, "Oh, Joel, I don't think I could ever get enough of you."

"Don't even try," he whispered encouragingly. He lifted onto one elbow and started kissing her back and shoulders, sliding his other hand under her to cup her breast. He squeezed it lightly, rhythmically, matching the steady silken rhythms of his other hand until Cassidy was moving urgently under him.

She tried to roll toward him but he held her gently, firmly, away from him and eased one knee between her thighs. He took his hand from her, murmuring quiet reassurance at her soft cry of loss, and showed her how to draw her knees up to make it easier for him. She gave another cry, this one of pure pleasure as he entered her with deep, swift certainty. She gasped his name as he started to move his hips, thinking for one incredible moment that she was going to burst into flame right there in his arms. Then just at the last, perfect instant, he went motionless.

He started kissing the nape of her neck, holding her so she couldn't move. As impossible as she would have thought it, the white-hot tension within her built even more, vibrating like a wire pulled so taut it had to snap. Then, when Cassidy was ready to faint with the sheer, exquisite agony of it, he started moving again, each short, rapid thrust sending an explosion of tremors ricocheting through her. She cried out and arched back toward him, feeling the same cataclysmic spasm shoot through Joel seconds later. He went taut and motionless, then collapsed against her with a groan.

Utterly spent, she closed her eyes and snuggled against him, body still joined sweetly with his. "What time is it?" she murmured sleepily.

"Don't know," came the drowsy, contented reply. "Don't care. Go back to sleep, darling."

She did, and awakened an hour or so later to find Joel propped up on one elbow beside her. He smiled. "What were you dreaming about? You were smiling in your sleep."

Cassidy laughed drowsily. "Can't you guess?" She slipped her arms around his neck. "We should get up sooner or later. We can't stay in bed all day."

"Like to put some money on that?" he murmured, kissing her lightly. "I should be exhausted, but you've done something to my regenerative powers I'd have thought impossible. I feel as though I could make love to you all day and all night, and still make my meeting in New York tomorrow morning ready to battle dragons."

"New York?"

Joel smiled at the disappointment in her voice. "Big meeting with my publisher. I'll be back Tuesday night in time to pick you up after *Headliners*, drag you home and make love to you until you beg me to stop."

"That could take a very long while indeed."

"That sounds like a challenge I can't pass up." He grinned and kissed the end of her nose, then sighed, stroking her breast thoughtfully. "There is one thing I have to do today, though. I try to get down to the Hutcheson to visit Jackie every couple of days, but with this damned book tour it's been nearly a week since I saw her last. I'll saddle one of the horses and you can take a ride around my mountain until I get back."

"Joel—" Cassidy lifted up on her elbow. "Would it be all right if I came along?" He frowned and she put her hand on his. "I'd like to be there with you. Jackie's an important part of your life, and I'd like to meet her."

Still frowning, he swept her hair back from her face. "She won't know we're there, you realize that, don't you?" Cassidy nodded, and Joel held her gaze for a moment or two. Then he tugged her into his arms with a quiet laugh. "You win! But first," he murmured, guiding her hand, "what do you suggest we do about this other matter?"

"Again?" she asked in astonishment.

"You have the most uplifting effort on me, Cassidy Yorke," he teased, catching his breath as she touched him with gentle fingers. "I think we're going to be a little late."

"You're late today, Joel," Dr. Katherine Salazar walked down the front steps of the Hutcheson clinic with a long, swinging stride, shading her eyes with one hand. "Hello, Miss Yorke. I'm glad you changed your mind about visiting us."

Cassidy smiled. "I hope you have time to give me that tour you promised. And please, call me Cassidy."

"I'd be delighted to show you around," Dr. Salazar looked at Joel. "Dr. Meistering's in my office. She flew in from Austria to show us the new awareness response therapy for coma patients that she's had such spectacular luck with. I think you'll find what she has to say interesting."

"I've been looking forward to meeting her ever since you told me about her." He squeezed Cassidy's hand. "Will you be all right by yourself for a few minutes?"

"Of course." She smiled. "Dr. Salazar is going to give me a tour. I'll see you later."

"Call me Katherine. I have a feeling we're going to be seeing a lot of you around here from now on." Cassidy gave her a startled look and Katherine laughed. "I've seen that silly expression on a man's face before. And if you'll excuse me for being blunt, it's exactly what he needs." She sighed, watching Joel disappear into the clinic. "I worry about him. Between his work and Jackie..." She gave her head a shake. "Well, come on. I hope you were serious about this tour, because I'm damned serious about our needing the publicity."

Cassidy fell into step beside Katherine as they walked up the steps to the clinic entrance. The Hutcheson looked more like a resort or private estate than a hospital, the brilliant white adobe-style walls, red tiled roof and sweeping crushed brick driveway fitting right in with the New Mexican landscape. It was set well back from the highway in the cool, sweet scented shade of a stand of pines, protected and peaceful behind its high wrought iron Spanish fence and arched gate. The entire place, like Katherine Salazar herself, radiated a calm competence that was restful and reassuring.

"I'll take you through the administration area here, then on to the labs, the rehabilitation and counseling areas and so on. Then I'll take you through the wards." Katherine gave Cassidy a speculative look. "Some people find it pretty depressing. There's a lot of despair here, a lot of tears. Most of the patients we get need care beyond what normal hospitals can provide—seniors who can no longer care for themselves, the terminally ill, people in the last stages of debilitating or progressively destructive diseases. Others—like Joel's sister—are in comas." She smiled suddenly, shoving her hands into the pockets of her white lab coat. "But there's hope, too. Bad cases go into remission. Coma patients waken one day for no apparent medical reason. Seniors suddenly discover a reason to live and become positively rejuvenated."

"What about Jackie Logan?" Cassidy asked quietly.

Katherine's face turned pensive. She shook her head. "In most cases, if a coma extends past a month, hope of recovery becomes vanishingly small. It happens, of course. No one knows why, or how, but it happens. But Jackie's condition has remained pretty much unchanged for over two and a half years. Common sense—my medical side—tells me it's hopeless; but the woman in me—the ever hopeful optimist—says I'll walk into her room one day and find her awake and laughing. If love could bring her out of it, there'd be no doubt she would recover. Joel has been fantastic through all of it. For the better part of the first year he came in every day, helping the physiotherapist with the exercises, talking and reading to her, trying everything he could think of to reach her. But the strain of being here every day and playing at being Logan Wilde was simply too much. I had to tell him one day that for his own sake he had to accept the reality of her condition, and get on with his life. I don't think he's accepted it entirely, but he's come to terms with it." She smiled again, looking at Cassidy. "You must be very special to him for him to bring you here. I'm glad he's found someone he can share this with. He's been completely alone with it for too long." She pushed open a swinging door, suddenly very businesslike again. "Now, this is the main administration section. This is where it all begins."

It was nearly two hours later when Katherine finally led Cassidy back to the main floor. She paused at the door to her office. "Well? What do you think?"

"I think I'd like to come back later this week with a camera crew," Cassidy replied quietly.

"I hoped you'd say that. Call me a day ahead to set things up." She thrust out her hand. "Thanks for coming, Cassidy. A lot of people won't come near a place like this. It reminds them too much of their own mortality, I guess. If you can help us, I thank you. If not..." She shrugged. "Well, we'll get our money some other way. Now, can you find Jackie's room by yourself, or do you want a gun bearer and guide?"

Cassidy laughed, returning Katherine's firm handshake. "I can find it. And thank you. For the tour, and for a good story. I'll make sure it gets told."

Katherine grinned recklessly, pushing her office door open. "I think there's a lot of me in you, Cassidy Yorke. And I think you'll do all right."

Cassidy heard Logan's voice as she neared the open door of Jackie's room. She stopped, not wanting to intrude, then smiled as she realized he was reading aloud from *Alice In Wonderland*. She stepped into the room silently. Logan was sitting with his back to the door, his voice changing from character to character as Alice, the Hatter and March Hare argued over their tea. Jackie was lying still and pale, eyes closed, mouth lifted at the corners in what may have been a faint smile. She was beautiful. Her features were small and perfect, her skin as delicate as fine English china. A torrent of raven-black hair tumbled across the pillow and around her shoulders.

She looked as though she'd just fallen asleep and Cassidy found herself holding her breath, waiting for her eyes to open. They would be blue, Cassidy knew, so deeply blue they would be almost violet, and they would be alive with mischief and laughter. Something suddenly caught in her throat and she had to swallow, feeling the sting of unexpected tears. Joel must have sensed her there, because he glanced around in mid-word. "Don't stop," she whispered, blinking rapidly. "It's one of my favorite stories."

Joel looked at his sister, his expression indescribably gentle. "It was Jackie's favorite, too. I read it to her so often when we were kids that she knew it by heart. I keep hoping that hearing it now will bring her back from wherever she's gone."

Not quite trusting her voice, Cassidy pulled the other chair nearer to the bed. She sat down and put her hand on his, trying not to wince when he grasped it fiercely.

"I spent half my life teasing her and bullying her and wishing she'd go away and leave me alone," he said very softly, his voice rough with emotion. "We only really got to know each other during her last year at college. All of a sudden she was grown-up, and I discovered she was a pretty fantastic person. Then I . . . lost her."

Cassidy tightened her fingers around his. "Read for a while longer, Joel," she whispered. "I could use a little anchoring at the moment myself."

"Rough?"

"Very." She took a deep breath. "My grandmother died last year. I was her favorite, the youngest and the only girl. She spoiled me terribly. And I absolutely adored her. She was always there for me, no matter what trouble I was in. I guess I thought she'd always be there for me." She had to stop to swallow, feeling the hot saltiness spill. "During the last few months she didn't know us. I could see the fear and confusion in her eyes and wanted so badly to comfort her, but she wouldn't let me touch her or even go near her. She didn't know who I was.'' Her chin trembled and she had to bite her lip to stop from sobbing aloud. ''I'm sorry,'' she finally managed to whisper. ''I thought I'd gotten over it.''

Joel swore softly, cradling her against him. ''I shouldn't have brought you here.''

''Oh, no!'' She wiped her cheek, smiling gamely. ''I wouldn't have missed it for the world. I've never been so impressed with anything in my life as I am with these people.''

''I love you, Cassidy Yorke,'' he murmured as he wiped a stray tear from her cheek. ''Remind me to show you just how much when we get back to the ranch.''

Ten

Well, well, Cassidy. Running a little late this morning, aren't we?'' Smiling, Marsh Wheeler paused by the coffee machine where Cassidy was pouring her first cup of the day.

She gave his expensive alpaca overcoat and fine leather gloves a pointed look. ''At least I made the production planning meeting this morning.''

''I make a habit of missing them whenever possible,'' Marsh replied calmly. ''I prefer to tell Vaughn what I'm going to do, not the other way around.'' His smile widened and he drew his hand from behind his back. ''For you,'' he announced, handing her a florist's bouquet of yellow long stemmed roses.

''Marsh!'' Cassidy looked at him in delight. ''They're gorgeous! But what on earth have I done to deserve roses?''

''Taking over for me at that dreary balloon rally on Saturday.'' He slipped his coat from his shoulders and folded it tidily over his arm. ''I simply could not face one of Vaughn's cheery little goodwill extravaganzas—not at that hour, at any rate. Rising before noon is barely tolerable at best; rising before dawn on a Saturday is not even *negotiable*!"

Cassidy laughed, breathing in the scent of roses. "Actually, I'm glad you changed your mind. It was fun."

"Hmm. So I gather." He raised an elegant eyebrow and leaned against the wall.

Cassidy simply smiled, pretending to be very interested in adding the right quantity of cream to the coffee.

"I hear you and Logan Wilde created quite a sensation among the paparazzi," he persisted. "Dashing off into the New Mexican wilds never to be heard of again. Both conspicuously absent at the banquet. Then Cassidy Yorke, the woman the entire station sets clocks by, the woman for whom punctuality is a moral sacrament, arrives for work an hour and a half late this morning." He smiled speculatively. "You and Wilde becoming an item?"

Cassidy had to laugh. "I can assure you, Marsh, that Logan Wilde and I are not becoming an item." Which wasn't quite a lie, she told herself as she picked up the coffee and roses and walked toward her desk. After all, she had fallen in love with Joel Logan this weekend, not with his alter ego. And it was Joel Logan, not Logan Wilde, who had ambushed her in the shower this morning before they had left the ranch and had coaxed her into one last hour of lovemaking. An hour's lovemaking, she remembered with a smile, that had made Joel very nearly miss his plane to New York and had made her miss a good half of Ken Vaughn's production planning meeting.

Cassidy's smile faltered, then vanished altogether as she thought of that morning's meeting. She took a sip of coffee and stared at the roses thoughtfully.

"Had I known they were going to depress you so badly, I'd have brought you chocolates."

Cassidy looked up blankly. Then she laughed, realizing that Marsh was sitting on the edge of the desk looking down at her. "Sorry. I was just thinking about the meeting."

"That bad?" He broke off a corner of the almond croissant that Cassidy had bought at the corner bakery.

"I just had a good idea shot down. Again."

"So." He nibbled at the pastry, then made a grimace of distaste and tossed it aside, wiping his fingers fastidiously on a paper napkin. "And what do you have lined up this week?"

"Earthshaking events, all," Cassidy muttered darkly. "A psychic fair, a man in Taos who says he's picking up messages from outer space on his electric razor, and an in-depth study of Albuquerque's after-work watering spots." She smiled wryly. "I suppose I should know better by now than to suggest anything remotely serious for *Cassidy's Corner*." She looked at Marsh for a long moment, then sat up, suddenly serious. "You know, you might be able to help me."

He smiled indulgently. "You need only ask, my beautiful one. If it's in the realm of possibility, it's yours."

She looked at him carefully. "I want you to persuade Ken Vaughn to let me do a show on the Hutcheson clinic."

He looked surprised. "What makes you think I can help?"

"Come on, Marsh!" she chided with a quiet laugh. "I don't know what you've got on Vaughn, but it's no secret that you pretty much get your way in terms of programming. When I presented my idea in this morning's meeting, it created some interest, but it got shot down anyway. But with a word of support from you, I think they'll let me do it."

"The Hutcheson?" Marsh gave his head a skeptical shake. He pulled out one of the slim imported cigarillos he enjoyed and lit it, inhaling deeply. "Odd topic."

"They do an incredible job, Marsh!" Cassidy sat forward. "It's the most advanced chronic care facility in the entire country. They've become the leading edge of a brand-new way of caring for the so-called 'hopeless' patients, the ones that fall through the cracks in the existing medical system. Their research labs are something out of a Spielberg movie, and they've got some of the top people in the field working on cures for everything from cancer to Alzheimer's disease. They've caught the attention of doctors everywhere. A week never goes by that a delegation from some country or another doesn't come through wanting to see what they're accomplishing."

"Sounds boringly upbeat," he teased. "What's the catch?"

"Money." She leaned back in the chair. "Colonel Hutcheson left them an endowment from the estate when he died, in memory of his wife. It's an ongoing thing—so much a year for the next zillion or so years. The problem is, no provision was made to cover inflation. They get the same annual endowment today that they were getting when they first opened in 1943. And you can imagine how far it goes. It barely covers daily expenses if no one gets extravagant, but they simply don't have the money they need for modernization, expansion or even new equipment. Even simple building maintenance is a major financial problem. Because they're low-profile—and because 'chronic care' isn't flashy or exciting like artificial hearts and organ transplants—they wind up on the bottom of everyone's funding list."

Marsh blew a smoke ring, watching it drift lazily over Cassidy's head. "And you think a story on KALB will help?"

"I *know* a story on KALB will help. Once people know how the work the clinic is doing touches us all, money will start pouring in!" Marsh smiled tolerantly and Cassidy laughed. "Well, maybe not pouring, exactly. But even a trickle will help."

He nodded, looking down at her thoughtfully. "Tell me something. What's your interest in this? Apart from the obvious humanitarian aspects, of course. I've seen you enthusiastic before, but I've never seen you this intense."

"I . . . spent some time there this weekend," she hedged.

"At the Hutcheson?" Again, she'd managed to surprise him. He looked at her curiously. Then he slipped off the desk and pulled out a chair, sitting down. "It may have possibilities. Tell me everything. Right from the beginning. Starting with why were you at the Hutcheson."

Cassidy frowned, tugging at a rose leaf. "I can't tell you that."

"It's got something to do with Logan Wilde, that much I've figured out."

"It doesn't have anything to do with Logan Wilde."

"Cass," Marsh sighed patiently. "This is Marsh Wheeler you're talking to, remember? You can trust me. I just want to know what's going on—how Wilde figures into it—in case you've gotten yourself mixed up in one of his publicity stunts."

"It isn't!" she protested indignantly. "Joel Logan is—" She caught herself. "Look, Marsh, I just can't tell you."

Marsh put his hand on hers. "Cassidy, you're asking me to risk my reputation for this story. Now I want to help you, but you've got to level with me. Logan Wilde's a hot topic these days. I don't want to go to Ken and persuade him to let you do this story, only to discover that Wilde's somehow using you to keep his name in the news." He held up his hand as she sucked in an outraged breath. "I know, I know—you're not new at this business. But admit it, you haven't been at it as long as I have, either. And when you *have* been in it as long as I have, you'll know why I'm not going to Ken until you tell me the story behind the story. All of it."

"Marsh..." Cassidy looked at him pleadingly. She couldn't tell him! Joel had told her the truth about Logan Wilde in absolute confidence; if the story got out, his career would be ruined.

"Cass, I'd like to help you, but..."

Cassidy felt panic rise as Marsh pushed back the chair and stood up. Damn it, she couldn't just let it go like this. Ken would never let her do the story. Even if she took a camera crew out to the Hutcheson and did the story without executive approval, it would never be aired. Marsh Wheeler was her only chance. She took a deep breath, praying that Joel would understand. "All right," she said softly. "I'll tell you everything. But Marsh, you have to promise me you won't breathe a word of this to anyone. I mean it—not a single soul is to find out what I'm going to tell you!"

Marsh sat down and held up his right hand solemnly. "I do so swear, Cassidy Yorke. Your terrible little secret will die with me."

Cassidy had to smile. "Sometimes, Marsh Wheeler, I'm very glad you went into television instead of politics. You have a flair for persuasion that's absolutely frightening." She took a deep breath, then, trying to tell herself that she was doing the right thing, she told him everything. About the Hutcheson. About Jackie. And about Logan Wilde. When she was finished, she looked up at him. Aside from asking her a couple of questions, he hadn't said a thing the entire time. He was still silent, staring contemplatively at the smoke rising from the end of his cigarillo.

"Well?" she urged. "Do you think it'll make a good story?"

His eyes flicked up to meet hers. "I think, Cass, my darling, that it'll make one hell of a story."

Cassidy's heart soared. "You'li talk to Ken?"

"Absolutely." Then he smiled and stood up. "But in the meantime, I have some work to do on tonight's show."

Cassidy nodded, watching Marsh walk away. She wished she didn't feel so horribly guilty, and wished Joel was home so she could talk to him. And tell him what, she asked herself unhappily. That it was scarcely four hours since they had last made love, and she had already betrayed him?

But it was the only way, she reminded herself wearily. Without Marsh's help she would never get the go-ahead for her documentary on the Hutcheson. A documentary that would help not only the clinic, but Joel and his sister, too.

Perhaps the medication or therapy that would help Jackie was just a few research dollars away.

Ken Vaughn was waiting for her when she came off the *Headliners* set after her show the next evening. She could see him pacing impatiently to one side and she thanked her guest again for coming, reminding him not to forget his electric razor. As he turned to leave, Cassidy cast the ceiling a grateful glance and smiled as she walked toward Ken.

"No alien contact tonight?"

"Not even an NBC football game." She smiled wryly. "He figures our transmission tower interfered with the signals."

"Our transmission tower is up in the Sandia Mountains."

"Details, details," Cassidy teased. "What's up?"

"The Hutcheson clinic," Ken replied in clipped tones. "What the hell's going on, Cass? You know better than to schedule a camera and sound crew for a project of that size without clearing it with me first."

Cassidy winced. "I guess I did jump the gun a little. I'm sorry, Ken, but I was hoping to get out there this Friday. And you know how hard it is to get a crew on short notice."

He stared at her in exasperation. "Yeah, yeah—but you still haven't answered my question! What are you doing out at the Hutcheson in the first place? Is this another one of your little free-lance efforts, like that Taos story?"

"That story on the water shortage in Taos was scheduled," Cassidy reminded him, annoyed by his tone.

"You were supposed to have been out there doing a story on native rain dances, not—"

"Which wouldn't be necessary at all if we weren't diverting water off Indian lands and into—"

"Hold it!" Ken held up both hands, silencing her. "No lectures on social responsibility, Cassidy. Just tell me what the hell you think you're doing out at the Hutcheson."

"Hasn't Marsh talked to you?"

"Marsh? Marsh talks to me every day, but he hasn't mentioned anything about doing a story on the Hutcheson."

"He isn't," Cassidy sighed. "I am. Damn! He said he was going to talk to you about it this morning." She took a deep breath, looking at Ken squarely. "Well, I guess the proverbial cat's out of the bag, so I may as well tell you about it. I was out at the Hutcheson this weekend—"

"Yeah, I know. You were out there with Wilde. Or Logan, or whatever the hell his real name is."

Something cold brushed the back of Cassidy's neck. "How—how do you know about that?" she asked very carefully.

"Wheeler told me, of course."

"So he *did* talk to you about the Hutcheson."

"Just briefly," Ken replied impatiently. "Only as it applies to his own story on—" Suddenly Ken stopped, staring at her. "Well, I'll be damned. You really don't have a clue, do you?" He gave an astonished laugh, shaking his head. "So that's what this is all about! Wheeler promised to talk to me about this story of yours, whatever it is, in return for all the dope on Wilde. Payment for all the work you did."

Cassidy frowned, shaking her head in bewilderment. "What are you talking about? Marsh said the Hutcheson story—"

"The Hutcheson story?" Ken gave a whoop of laughter. "God, you're naive! Did you really believe that Marsh Wheeler gives a damn about your little story? Or you? It was Wilde's story he wanted, Cassidy!"

"Wilde's story?" she echoed faintly.

Ken looked at her pityingly. "He set it up right from the beginning. Whose idea do you think it was to have Wilde on *Headliners* in the first place? Wheeler knew there was a story there somewhere. He spent nearly three weeks trying to track it down, but couldn't even get close. So he turned you loose on it. He gambled that a woman, the right woman, would get through Wilde's defenses. All he had to do was wait for you to uncover Wilde's little secret, whatever it was, then reel you—and the story—in."

Cassidy stared at Ken numbly, too shocked to do more than blink stupidly at him. "I—I don't believe it," she finally managed to say in a ragged whisper.

"Why do you think you took Wheeler's place at the balloon rally? He figured if he kept throwing the two of you together, something would happen. I guess it finally did."

"He wouldn't..." whispered Cassidy brokenly.

"No?" Ken smiled. "Then I guess you won't be interested in Wheeler's show tonight. It's a big exposé about a mediocre writer named Joel Logan."

Cassidy recoiled as though he had struck her. "No," she moaned, paling so suddenly she felt light-headed. She gave her head a shake of denial, starting toward the set. "Oh, my God, no!"

"It's too late, you little fool!" Ken snatched her arm and spun her around. "He's dug it all up, Cassidy. You gave him the key he needed, and he got it all. He's going to crucify Logan out there tonight. It's Wheeler's kind of show—the dirty, back stabbing kind of stuff he thrives on."

"And you let him do it?" Shock was giving away to anger now. Anger, and a sick sense of unreality. "How could—?"

"Because Marsh Wheeler owns me, that's why!" Ken snarled. "Heart and soul! I made some mistakes a few years ago, dumb kid mistakes. It was my first television job. I was living the role to the hilt—and I got involved with drugs." His nostrils flared. "I stopped, but Marsh found out about it somehow. When NBC fired him two years ago, he couldn't get a job anywhere. So he started calling in his debts. I was one of them. I was already working here, he needed a job..." He shrugged. "If Crothers finds out about my background, I'm finished at KALB."

"I can't believe this," Cassidy whispered in shock.

Ken gave a bark of harsh laughter. "Who the hell do you think's been holding you back these past ten months? Crothers? Crothers thinks you're the hottest thing since Johnny Carson! It's been Wheeler, baby! Marsh Wheeler, the ego that walks like a man: your friend, your mentor. He's the real exec producer at this station. I'm just the puppet, jumping when he pulls the strings." He grinned savagely. "You scare the hell out of him, Cassidy. He had it made here. He built himself a nice little empire, calling the tunes and watching everyone dance. It isn't quite New York, but an empire's an empire. Then you came along, a young hotshot ex-weather forecaster from some backwoods Oregon station who suddenly started coming up fast on the inside track. You're good, Cass, damned good. Wheeler knows that if anyone finds out just *how* good, he's through. And KALB's about the end of the trail for him. There aren't many more places for him to go."

Cassidy put her hand on the edge of the desk to steady herself, wondering if she was going to faint. This was impossible. It wasn't happening. "Why—" Her throat was so dry she had to swallow. "Why are you telling me this now?"

He stared at her. "Damned if I know, Cassidy. Maybe I'm tired of watching you batter your head against a brick wall."

But Cassidy was only half listening. She was staring toward the *Headliners* set. "We've got to stop him."

"It's too late," Ken said softly. "It's nearly over."

"No!" She spun away from Ken's restraining hand and sprinted toward the back stairs leading up to the control booth, ignoring the startled stares and murmurs following her. *You've got to stop him!* she chanted to herself as she raced up the stairs. *Oh, please, let me be in time to stop him!*

She burst into the control room. Two or three people glanced around, then turned their attention back to their control boards. Cassidy walked to the main board. Dick Craig had his back to her, watching the wall of monitor screens in front of him. Cassidy knew that the one labeled

Program showed him what was being transmitted at that instant, while the one marked *Preview* showed him his next shot. Under these large two monitors were six smaller screens, the three on the left showing him what each of the three cameras was actually "seeing," the others showing him pre-taped material, superimposed titles and so on that he would "roll in" when he wanted them as he put the show together.

"Wider pan," Dick was murmuring into his headset mike. "Take three, tighten up, take one, zoom out. Hurry out, Camera Three—give me Wheeler tight. Two, get wide—wider. Take two. Music in..."

The entire place resembled a Tokyo street in rush hour, although Cassidy knew the chaos and seemingly conflicting chatter of voices and commands were more apparent than real. It always unnerved her slightly to come up here, but at this moment she was interested only in one thing. She stepped beside Dick, ignoring his startled glance, and stared up at the *Program* monitor. Marsh was smiling into the camera, his mouth moving silently. "What's he saying?" she asked urgently.

"What the—?" The associate director glared around at Cassidy. "Get her out of here!"

"Cassidy!" One of the production assistants drew her gently back from the monitors. "You shouldn't be in here!"

"What's he saying?" she demanded again, snatching a headset out of his hand. She held it to one ear, heart pounding.

"...biggest put-on of the twentieth century," he was saying. "Logan Wilde, or should I say Joel Logan, is a spoof—a parody of that thing we hold so sacred: the 'expert.' We abound in them these days. They pop up every time we turn around—experts at this, experts at that. And now we have the best of all: the 'expert expert.' The fact he's managed to fool us all for two and a half years is, I suppose, a comment on our society. Are we really so starved for advice, so desperate to be told the 'truth,' that we'll let a writer of not very good western novels dictate every move of our sex lives, right down to the last—''

Cassidy flung the headset away from her and stepped beside Dick. ''Stop him! You've got to cut him off!''

''Are you crazy?'' someone hissed. ''It's already over!''

''You don't understand—''

''George, get her the hell out of here!''

''Come on, Cass.'' Someone pulled her away from the control board by the arm. She was shaking now, so cold with rage and betrayal that she felt sick. ''Oh, Joel,'' she whispered. ''Joel, what have I done?'' Suddenly she wheeled around to look at the big clock over the monitors. He was flying in from New York tonight. In fact, she had been going to call him right after the show. If he'd watched her tonight, if his television was still on and he was watching Marsh right now. . . !

She was out the control room door and down the stairs like a deer. She burst into the dressing room and dialed Joel's number, her hand trembling so badly she had to try twice before getting it right.

''Answer,'' she whispered pleadingly, listening to it ring. ''Please, Joel, be there. Answer . . . please!'' The receiver at the other end was lifted, and she gave a gasp of relief. ''Oh, thank God! Joel—Joel, you've got to listen to—''

''Well, well. If it isn't little Miss Television herself.'' It was Joel's voice, so cold and controlled that it could have been a stranger's. ''Hello, Cassidy. Calling to see how I liked the show?''

''Joel, listen to me! It isn't what you think!''

''No?'' He laughed, a quiet chilling sound. ''You're good, Cassidy. God, you're good! I swallowed it all, sweetheart—hook, line and sinker! If you ever get tired of playing the zoo circuit, you should think about a career on the stage. Or in the secret service. With a technique like yours, there wouldn't be a government secret left untouched.''

''Joel!'' Cassidy squeezed the receiver so hard her hand ached. ''Joel, I love you! All this is a horrible mistake—''

"Love!" He gave a snort of bitter laughter. "Give it up, darling. You got your story. They'll probably make you executive producer for this one. Just one thing bothers me. Why did you let Wheeler go on the air with it? Or were you both in on it? That would explain why you just happened to turn up at the balloon rally on Saturday, wouldn't it?"

"No," she moaned. "Oh, Joel, it's not like that at all! Please, listen to me. I wanted to do a story on the Hutcheson—"

"Yeah, I know. Katherine called me a few minutes ago, saying you'd been in touch with them. Is that what this was all about, Cass? Was your story on me just collateral, just the thirty pieces of silver you paid to get your show format changed?"

"No, I—"

"I hope it wasn't too distasteful," he went on, his voice cold and remote. "Did you enjoy it, Cass? Or was it just one of those things you were willing to endure to get ahead? You seemed to like it—or was that part of the act, too? What were you thinking about when we made love, Cass? Your next show? Your next victim? Are you going to make love with him, too? Are you going to say the things to him you said to me?"

"Joel!" It was a heartbroken sob and Cassidy had to fight to speak through sudden, hot tears. "Joel, you can't believe that!"

"You said you always like to win. I guess I just underestimated how badly. It's a dirty business, but you've obviously learned how to play the game. You'll do well, kid. Until you meet someone a little more ruthless, a little more hungry."

"Joel!" Cassidy sobbed. "Please!"

Then, softly, gently, he put down the receiver. The line went dead with brutal finality and Cassidy listened to the dial tone, feeling the tears stream down her cheeks. "No," she whispered. "Oh, God, this can't be happening! Joel, I love you!"

"Lover's spat, darling?" came a dry, laughing voice from just behind her. "He'll get over it. They always do."

Cassidy stiffened. Not turning around, she put the receiver back into its cradle gently. She took a deep, slow breath. "Why?" she whispered. "Can you at least tell me that?"

"Why?" Marsh echoed thoughtfully. "Because it made a good story, that's why. If you had a brain in that beautiful head of yours, you'd have kept it for yourself instead of handing it to me on a silver platter. Not," he added with a self-congratulatory chuckle, "that I'm complaining."

"You bastard." Struggling to control her rage, Cassidy turned around slowly. "You manipulative, amoral, self-serving bastard! You just destroyed a man's life tonight, do you realize that? Does that bother you, Marsh? Do you feel the slightest remorse? The tiniest bit of guilt?"

"No." He stared back at her with cool derision. "That's the difference between us, Cassidy. You're still trying to be a nice person. Sweet Cass, everybody's friend. And they adore you, Cass. There isn't a man or woman in this place who wouldn't walk through fire for you." His mouth twisted into a sneer. "God, how I loathe that syrupy, cheerful smile of yours!"

"My God," she whispered, sickened and stunned with shock. "To think I once looked up to you! To think I actually trusted you, wanted to be like you!"

"Oh, you are, darling! You are! I'm the only one who's seen through the holier-than-thou act, of course, but down deep you're no different from me." His smile vanished. "You manipulate people to get what you want just like I do, darling, so don't look at me as though I make you sick. Do you think I don't know how you got this story? I may have used you, Cass, but at least I didn't sleep with you to get my story." He smiled mockingly. "You might have rationalized it by convincing yourself that you love Joel Logan, but the truth is that you just used the best bait to bring in the fish. If you really loved him, you wouldn't have sold him out for a dozen Hutcheson stories. Face it, Cassidy—you made a conscious choice between your career and betraying the man you slept with. And your career won." His smile widened. "Maybe there's hope for you, yet."

"That's not true," she whispered. "I did it for Joel."

Marsh smiled drolly. "If that's true, you're in big trouble. There's no room in this business for nice people. If you're not man enough to go for the jugular, Cass, find yourself another job. Because it's every man for himself out here. Be nice, and you'll just get swallowed alive."

Cassidy stared at him, unable to believe that she could feel such total, umremitting rage and yet be so completely helpless. "You poor, pathetic little man," she whispered. "How can you face yourself in the mirror every day?" Turning away before he could see her tears, she picked up her leather jacket and handbag and stepped by him and out the door.

Behind her, he laughed softly. "Oh, you'll learn, darling," he promised her. "You'll learn."

Eleven

She had to talk with Joel! Still blinking back tears, Cassidy put her little MGB in gear. The tires gave a squeal of protest as she shot out of her parking spot and into the street. If she could just talk to him, just explain, everything would be all right, she told herself as she headed the small car toward Joel's apartment. He had every right to be angry with her. What must have gone through his head when Marsh's segment of *Headliners* had come on? It must have left him as stunned and hurt as it had left her, thinking she had betrayed him, that those long, exquisite hours of lovemaking had been nothing more than a game to her.

Naive, Ken had called her. Cassidy gave a sob of tearful laughter. Naive! The word didn't even begin to describe how incredibly blind she'd been all these months, how unbelievably gullible. She had played into Marsh's manipulative hands like a trusting child, not even suspecting that it was he and not Ken who was responsible for keeping her on the zoo circuit. He knew her; he knew that eventually she would simply quit KALB in frustration, leaving his little empire unthreatened.

She had even helped him with his plan. How many times had she confided in him? How many great ideas had she bounced off him, only to have them shot down in the planning meeting later? She couldn't have been a more helpful victim. And this last move had been the most perfectly orchestrated of all. She'd done his research and leg work, she had uncovered his story. Then she'd handed him the entire thing, giftwrapped and tied with a big red bow.

She had to explain that to Joel. He had to understand that she hadn't done it with intent or malice. He had to listen to her. She wouldn't leave until he listened to her.

"I'm sorry, Miss," the concierge was saying nearly twenty minutes later, "but you'll have to leave. Mr. Wilde does not wish to be disturbed."

"You don't understand." Cassidy forced herself to stay calm. "It is absolutely imperative that I see him. Please call him up again and tell him it's Cassidy Yorke. He must have misunder—"

"No misunderstanding, Miss. You'll have to leave now." He stood between her and the elevators like the retired Marine sargeant he probably was, impeccably polite, utterly unmoved.

How many adoring Logan Wilde fans had he held off single-handedly, Cassidy found herself wondering. How many other distraught women had stood here trying to tearfully convince him that it was a matter of life and death that they see Logan Wilde? No wonder he looked amused and mildly bored.

Fighting growing panic, she gritted her teeth to keep from screaming at him in sheer frustration. "Look, will you please just let me talk with him? Ring him again, that's all I'm asking."

"I'm sorry, Miss," he repeated obdurately. "If you don't leave the premises, I'm going to have to call Security." He suddenly leaned toward her. "Please, Miss Yorke," he added with unexpected gentleness, "don't make me get official. We've had television and newspaper people here all evening, and Mr. Wilde's not seeing anyone. Maybe tomorrow."

"But I'm not here in an official capacity!" she said urgently. "This hasn't got anything to do with KALB, don't you understand? I have to talk with him! Please, call him again and he'll explain—"

"I've called him twice now," he replied, gentleness evaporating under growing impatience. "And he says he doesn't want to see you. Now I'm going to ask you once more to leave, Miss Yorke. I won't ask again."

"But—" She stopped, realizing by his expression that he was deadly serious about having her physically removed from what was very obviously *his* lobby. She nodded dumbly and turned away, tears spilling as she made her way blindly out to the car. Now what, she wondered hopelessly, feeling so cold and empty it was all she could do to keep her teeth from chattering as shiver after shiver racked her.

Somehow she made her way back to her own apartment, driving through a haze of tears most of the way. Not even bothering to turn on the lights, she undressed and curled up under the hand stitched quilt her grandmother had made. She hugged Sam against her, desperately needing the touch and warmth of something alive. But even Sam's furry, purring warmth couldn't ease the chills and she lay staring wide-eyed in the darkness, shivering uncontrollably.

This couldn't be happening. Two nights ago she had been lying in Joel's arms, filled with the warmth of him, sharing the most beautiful, breathtaking magic possible between a man and a woman. Tonight, he was a stranger. She'd destroyed everything.

She closed her eyes against a flood of hot, salty tears and Sam gave a soft meow of protest as Cassidy's arms tightened convulsively. Marsh was right. She was no better than he was. Joel had told her the truth about Logan Wilde in absolute confidence. She had had no business breathing a word of it to Marsh or to anyone else. But she'd let her job—that damned job!—seduce her into breaking that confidence. Oh, she had convinced herself that she was doing it all for Joel, but the truth was that she'd done it for herself. She had let the possibility of doing a documentary on the Hutcheson blind her to right and wrong. She'd bartered Joel's trust like a bauble at a country fair.

Sam gave another meow of complaint and wriggled free of Cassidy's grasp. Tail twitching, she leapt down and stalked out of the bedroom. In spite of her misery, Cassidy had to smile. She was really doing great tonight—she had managed to antagonize not only the man she loved, but poor Sam as well. She sighed and got up, clutching the quilt around her shoulders as she walked into the kitchen. A tin of food and a bowl of warm milk would make amends with Sam.

Making amends with Joel wouldn't be that easy. She frowned as she opened the tin of cat food, trying not to step on Sam's toes as the hungry cat pirouetted anxiously. Perhaps it would be impossible. She hadn't simply hurt Joel; she had betrayed his secret. The networks would have picked up the story by now. By tomorrow morning there wouldn't be a person in the country who didn't know that Logan Wilde was a fraud. Mystique gone, he was finished. But that was only part of it. Worse, the book contracts and talk shows and magazine columns that brought in the necessary income to keep Jackie at the Hutcheson would be finished, too.

Cassidy closed her eyes, shoulders sagging in defeat as she started to comprehend the enormity of what she'd done.

"I've got to make it right," she whispered to Sam, unable to stop the tears from welling again. "But how, Sam? What am I going to do!"

There was, really, only one thing *to* do, Cassidy realized the following evening as she waited for her cue. It was so simple, so obvious, that she gave a little laugh, wondering why on earth she hadn't seen it earlier. It wouldn't even begin to make up for the mistake she'd made, of course; but then, nothing could. All she could do now was make some small token gesture of apology, some small offering that just might bring some good out of this nightmare after all. And maybe, in some odd way, she had to do it as much for herself as for Joel.

She glanced up at the clock. Twenty minutes to air-time. No time to clear it with Dick Craig, but perhaps it was better that way. He and his technical team were good, good enough to wing it without a script or even advance warning, and the less they knew about this, the better it would be for them afterward. When they all got hauled up onto the carpet in Jack Crothers' office to explain what amounted to wholesale mutiny, they could plead ignorance. Besides, she reminded herself with a grim smile, the fewer people who knew about it, the better were her chances of staying on-air long enough for it to matter. One inkling of what she was up to, and Ken Vaughn would have her cut off and replaced with a pre-taped show so quickly that not a viewer in the whole of New Mexico would realize what had happened.

She took a deep breath and set her interview notes to one side, feeling a tiny thrill of excitement shoot through her. It was just a fleeting feeling, but it was a *feeling*—some sign that she was alive after all, that this bone-chilling numbness wasn't going to be permanent. She looked around her with faint interest, slowly becoming aware of her surroundings for the first time all day. She had gotten through this day one shaky step at a time, playing her role as Cassidy Yorke so flawlessly that no one had even noticed that she was just a hollow, brittle shell, afraid even to move too quickly in case she simply shattered into a thousand pieces.

"Fifteen minutes, Cass!"

Cassidy gave Mike Szaski a weak smile of acknowledgment. Fifteen minutes. Enough time to try to call Joel again. She gave the telephone a yearning glance, then sighed and resisted the temptation. It was no use. She would simply get a recorded message, as she had the last half-dozen times she called. Either he had gone into active hiding from reporters, or he simply wasn't answering the telephone. And if he did answer, she reminded herself pointedly, what would she say? What was left to say?

"Good newscast tonight, Cassidy."

Cassidy looked up. Ken was standing by the desk, his expression guarded, almost wary. His eyes met and held hers for a taut instant, and she knew he was thinking about yesterday. It had been between them all day, rank as smoke. He was different today somehow. Gone was the easy familiarity, the teasing, the smoothness. He looked weary and disillusioned, his face older than it had been a day ago. And suddenly, in spite of her anger, she felt sorry for him. Like her, he'd been forced to take a long, hard look at himself; like her, he hadn't particularly liked what he'd seen.

He let his gaze run over her thoughtfully, taking in the elegantly simple lines of her pale blue linen suit, the sleek chignon, the subdued makeup. "Are you going to change for your show?"

"No." She held his gaze almost defiantly. *No more games,* she told him silently. *I'm through with games.*

He nodded silently. One corner of his mouth turned up for an instant as though in silent acknowledgment of this final rebellion, and in that split second of eye contact, Cassidy thought: *he knows!* Someone called his name and he glanced around. When he looked back at Cassidy there was nothing in his expression to indicate what he'd been thinking.

He smiled, his eyes holding hers. "Have a good show tonight, Cass." Then he turned and walked away.

"I will," she murmured to his retreating back. "Yes, I think I will."

"Cass. Cass? Cassidy! Hey, lady, you with us tonight?"

"What?" Cassidy looked around at Mike. Then she smiled and stood up. "Yeah, I'm with you, Mike. Sorry. I was just thinking about something. Is Marsh in yet?"

"Came in a couple of minutes ago." Mike fell into step beside her and they walked toward the set together. "There a problem between you two? Seems to be a lot of tension in the air today, Cass—bad vibes going around like a virus."

Cassidy's shoulders tightened with anger. She forced herself to relax. "We've had a . . . disagreement."

"Better get it fixed," he suggested bluntly. "Something like that's hard to hide on-air."

"It won't be a problem for much longer, Mike," she told him calmly. "Count on it."

Something in her voice made him look at her sharply. Forcing herself to smile, she patted his shoulder reassuringly. "They're giving us the two minute sign. We've got a show to put on, remember?"

Cassidy was surprised at how calm she felt as she took her place on the *Headliners* set. She seemed just slightly apart from it all, as though the dollying cameras, the brilliant lights and the scurrying shadows weren't part of her immediate reality. Even being seated beside Marsh Wheeler didn't bother her. She looked squarely at him as she took her chair, then dismissed him as though he wasn't even worthy of her attention. His mouth tightened, and Cassidy felt a small flicker of satisfaction. She was relieved at how calmly she was handling it, because privately she'd been dreading this moment all day. Marsh had been strutting around the studio like a lord since coming in that morning. His show on Joel had brought him a brief flurry of attention and he had been lapping it up like a cat with cream, filled with his own cleverness. But right at the moment, he looked worried. Cassidy smiled to herself. It wasn't the show that had him concerned—it was her. Her private smile widened. *Sit there and stew about it!*

In spite of the tension between them, the three minute introduction went smoothly. Her teasing may have been more barbed than usual, but no one seemed to notice. Except for Marsh. His eyes were glittering with real anger when the camera prompting light went off.

"Don't push your luck," he murmured to her as he removed his mike. "If bad chemistry jeopardizes the show, remember which of us is more senior, all right?"

"Maybe we should leave that to Jack Crothers," she suggested pleasantly. Marsh's head shot around. He gave her a hard stare, and Cassidy, uncharacteristically pleased that her shot had found a sensitive spot, simply smiled.

"You're on, Cass," Mike cued her a few moments later. "Right... now!" The red light on Camera One blinked on.

Panic. In that split second, Cassidy froze. She stared into the camera, her mind suddenly blank, the sheet of paper with its hasty scribbles crumpled in one clenched fist. Her throat closed, and she wondered for a dazed instant if she was going to faint. Then, suddenly, instinct took over.

"Hello, again." She smiled warmly, a feeling of utter calm and peace washing through her as she fell into the comforting routine. "As you know, my guest tonight was to have been Judy Gilland, proprietor of the Sherlock Holmes book store. Unfortunately, Ms. Gilland couldn't be with us tonight." There was a rustle of confusion in the shadows around her. From the corner of her eye, Cassidy could see Judy Gilland—who was standing just off-camera, all prepared to walk onto the set—looking around in bewilderment. Mike was staring at her, mouth hanging open in astonishment. "I made a mistake last night," she continued candidly, ignoring the startled activity around her. "I broke a confidence, and broke someone's trust in me. There's a very special man out there tonight who thinks I betrayed him. I didn't intend it to happen that way, and it's too late now to say I'm sorry. Even if I did, mere words couldn't heal the hurt I've caused. So tonight's show is for him, and for what he believes in. And maybe in a way it's for me, too, and for what I believe in."

Ken had appeared from nowhere, white-faced, speaking urgently to Mike. Mike spoke rapidly into his headset as he looked over Cassidy's head to the control room and Cassidy swallowed, knowing they could cut her off at any instant. Perhaps they already had—no, the light on Camera One was still red. Only the camera operators seemed unconcerned by her mutiny. Ignoring the excited babble around them, they kept the cameras on her. The only thing that would interrupt them was a direct order from the control room. An order that could come through at any instant.

Just then the prompt light went out. Her heart plummeted in that eyeblink of time before she realized that Dick had simply switched her to Camera Two. She made the transition, blocking out everything but that staring camera lens. "I'm going to tell you about a very special place I visited this weekend—the Hutcheson clinic. Most of you are probably aware of the recent fund-raising rally held for the Hutcheson; some of you may have attended, many of you probably made donations. But I wonder how many of you really know what goes on there. What is the Hutcheson Chronic Care Facility? Who are these people, and what are they doing? Three days ago I didn't know the answers, either. Three days ago, I didn't care. But I care now. And I want you to care. So stay with me while I tell you why."

Cassidy didn't know where the words came from. They welled up from somewhere deep within her and she simply let them flow, talking quietly and steadily into first one camera then the other as Dick moved smoothly from angle to angle. She spoke with quiet urgency, focusing her attention completely on her audience as though she could somehow reach out and touch them. The babble around her faded and soon she wasn't even aware of the cameras or lights as she talked about Katherine Salazar and the rest of the staff, about the hope that was never lost, the tears, the laughter. She told them about the geriatric wards filled with freshly cut flowers and sunshine. About how an experimental program that filled those silent rooms with laughing children and pets from a nearby school was making such startling progress in rehabilitating the aged that it had electrified experts throughout the world. She talked about the cases that had been brought in labeled as hopeless, and how hope had been rekindled. She talked about the level of care, and the level of caring, about the unfaltering dedication among the staff, the quiet determination to make a difference.

She spoke with quiet but fluent urgency, knowing that she could be cut off at any instant and determined to make every second count. Gradually, she realized that the studio had fallen strangely silent. She could see Jeri standing as though mesmerized in the shadows behind the lights. Mike was standing beside her, his expression a peculiar blend of emotions that Cassidy didn't even dare try to translate. He, too, seemed strangely still, a sheaf of papers dangling by his side as though forgotten. Others were there: a handful of stagehands, usually busy elesewhere, a script assistant who was watching intently, eyes strangely bright, electricians and prop men, a couple of people that Cassidy thought worked in sales.

Ten minutes, and she was still on-air. As her internal clock told her they were nearing the halftime commercial break, she glanced instinctively at Mike. He shook his head almost imperceptibly and, to her astonishment, gave her the signal to continue. It startled her so badly that she very nearly missed her cue when Dick switched cameras. Had they lost their minds? The sales department—which would have to answer to the advertisers who had paid huge sums of money for those three one-minute spots that had just been cancelled—would be foaming at the mouth! Not to mention the legal department, which was probably already combing its FCC regulations and union contracts to see how many lawsuits they were facing.

But she kept talking, offering silent thanks to whoever was on her side up in that glassed-in control room. Finally, as Mike started counting down the seconds left, she made one more plea for donations. Then, throat raw, she looked straight into Camera One. "Before I sign off tonight, I'd like to thank everyone who has helped make *Cassidy's Corner* such a success over the past ten months. The camera operators and stagehands who hold everything together; the production staff; Dick Craig, the best director anyone could have; the dozens of other people here at KALB who come through night after night. And you, the audience that has made it all possible." She smiled. "After all, without you, nothing else really matters. I've been very lucky working here at KALB among some of the most talented people I've ever known. But everything has to come to an end. Even *Cassidy's Corner*. This is my last night with KALB." There was a shocked inhalation around her, a rising murmur of surprise. She ignored it. "I resigned this afternoon, for personal reasons. But I'd just like to say thanks. I'm going to miss you." The light went dead. There was utter silence, and Cassidy closed her eyes, sinking back into the chair. It was over.

She opened her eyes and unclipped her microphone, feeling drained. In the darkness, someone started to applaud. Someone else took up the lead, then another and another until soon the entire studio was clapping and cheering. Taken by surprise, Cassidy looked around uncertainly.

"Cassidy, that was fantastic!" Jeri told her as she wiped at her cheeks. "The phones haven't stopped ringing since two minutes into the show—people wanting to know why you haven't been doing shows like this right from the beginning. They've been calling Crothers, too. Everyone loved it!"

"Great show, Cass!" someone else shouted from the mob of people crowding around her. "Terrific!" someone else agreed exuberantly, giving her a fierce hug. "I cried like a baby! You can't be serious about quitting."

Cassidy worked her way toward the dressing room. Ken was standing by the door. He pushed it open for her, then pulled it firmly shut to close out the babble of excited voices and shouts of congratulations following her. "You seem to be a hit," he said. "The switchboard's going crazy. Someone from the Hutcheson phoned a couple of minutes ago and wants to talk with you. Seems their phones have been ringing off the wall with people wanting to make donations. Congratulations."

Cassidy looked at him. "You knew I was going to do that, didn't you? Why didn't you cut me off? You had lots of time."

But Ken simply smiled, turning toward the door. "Jack Crothers wants to see you before you leave tonight. He's probably going to give you a raise."

Cassidy pulled on her coat wearily, managing a faint smile. "I don't work here anymore, remember?"

"Give it some thought, Cass," he said quietly, pulling the door open.

"Ken . . . ?" He glanced around. "Thanks."

His smile widened for a fleeting moment, then he stepped through the door. "Good night, Cassidy."

The phone rang, startling her. She stared at it, then picked up her handbag and walked to the door. It was still ringing as she left the building and walked out into the cool night air.

The phone started ringing again. Cassidy closed the book on her finger and looked up at the bedroom door as though she could see through it, waiting. She could hear her father's firm tread cross the kitchen floor. There was a pause, then her mother's voice calling, "Who is it, dear?"

"New Mexico." Cassidy imagined she could hear her father sigh. "Again. Where's Cass?"

"In her room. Do you want me to call her?"

"No. When she's ready to talk to them, she'll talk. She has their number."

Cassidy smiled. Her father never complicated things unnecessarily. The fact his only daughter had come home two weeks ago without a word of explanation, or that the phone hadn't stopped ringing since, didn't bother him. He knew all he had to know. There had been some problem; she'd come home to work it out. When she was ready to talk about it, she would talk about it. And until then, he was quite content just to have her home again.

Cassidy set the book aside and rolled off the bed. She wandered across to the window and stared out across the back yard, past the flagstone patio that her father and brothers had spent an entire summer building, past the row of apple trees her grandfather had planted over thirty years ago, past her mother's rose beds and vegetable garden. The hills beyond rose wild and rugged against the sky, their thick growth of trees creating a million shades of green. The air, filled with birdsong and the soothingly familiar sound of the lawnmower, was tart with the cool scent of mountains and freshly cut grass. Steve, her youngest brother, strode into view pushing the lawnmower. He had taken his shirt off and tied it around his waist, and she could see the sun gleam on his sunbronzed back as he skillfully maneuvered the mower along the scalloped edge of the rose bed. For some reason, seeing him made her think of Joel Logan.

As it always did, the unexpected memory made her stomach twist. She rested her forehead on the cool glass, closing her eyes. Time was supposed to heal all wounds, she thought despairingly. When was it going to heal this one? When was she going to be free of his memory, of the sick guilt that flooded through her every time her mind turned traitorously to the past? She couldn't go on like this. She couldn't spend the rest of her life wandering numbly from day to day, bereft of joy or laughter, waiting, always waiting, for the unhappiness to lift. And she couldn't spend the rest of her life here, cocooned in her parent's house as though by returning she could actually turn time back, as though in this room, surrounded by the tangible artifacts of childhood, she could become that carefree child again, cared for and protected from hurt.

Because it wasn't working. Her father couldn't kiss this hurt away. Her mother couldn't ease the pain by baking a double recipe of chocolate brownies. This was her own hurt, an adult hurt, and she was going to have to face it by herself.

The phone rang again, making her jump. She looked at her white Princess extension, tempted to answer it, then wheeled away from the window and grabbed up her suede wind-breaker instead. She ran lightly down the stairs, detouring through the family room on her way to the back door. Her mother was standing in the middle of the room, high-kicking to a raucous disco beat as she followed the energetic gyrations of the televised aerobics instructor.

She saw Cassidy and stopped, blushing prettily, her face lightly sheened with perspiration and incredibly pretty under the mop of curly chestnut hair. "There has got to be a better way!" she protested with a laugh, picking up a towel and wiping her forehead. She patted her trim leotard-clad hips. "I don't know why your father and Steve can eat like wolves and never gain an ounce, and all I have to do is walk by a bakery and inhale deeply to put on a pound."

"Genetics," Cassidy sympathized with a laugh. "Why didn't you tell me it was on, and I'd have joined you. I could use a good workout myself."

"How about tomorrow morning—if you don't mind getting teased mercilessly. Steve and your father seem to find the whole thing hilarious." She tossed the towel aside and turned off the television. "How about a cup of coffee? I just made a fresh pot for your father."

"Maybe later. I thought I'd go riding for a while."

Her mother nodded. "I suppose you didn't get much chance to go horseback riding in Albuquerque."

"No." Cassidy looked away abruptly, remembering that Sunday afternoon when Joel had given her a horseback tour of his ranch. They'd stopped beside a creek and had made love in the sun dappled shadows of a giant pine, lying naked in each other's arms for hours afterward, talking and laughing and making love again. "I'll see you later."

Twelve

The grove hadn't changed. The tall pines rose like pillars, solid as time itself, the ground beneath them spongy with needles and moss and tiny trembling ferns. The rock face, too, was unchanged. Wet and mossy, it rose from the rust-colored ground like the ruins of some pagan temple. Water gushed down the glittering stone and into the obsidian pond at its foot. The overflow rushed merrily into the far meadow where it eventually lost itself in marsh. It was cool and still under the trees. Cassidy straddled the ancient fallen log that jutted out over the pond and leaned forward until she was resting on her elbows, staring down into the inky water.

She'd come out here on a whim, hoping that the glade still held the answers it had when she was a child. She had always come out here when troubled or undecided about something, and it had rarely failed her. But somehow she didn't think that childhood magic was going to work this time.

KALB wanted her back. Ken had quit the day after her show, taking a job with a small station in New Orleans. Marsh was gone too. Jeri thought he was working a late morning spot on a Canadian Broadcasting Corporation radio station somewhere in northern Saskatchewan.

Jeri phoned nearly every day, asking Cassidy to reconsider her resignation. Even Jack Crothers himself had called once, sounding gruff and embarrassed. She had told him what she'd been telling Jeri: that she needed time to think. Strangely, he had seemed to understand. "Take your time," he'd told her. "Don't do anything that doesn't feel right."

Other stations had been calling, too. Seattle. Vancouver. San Francisco. Dallas. A handful of tiny places she'd never heard of until now. They had all seen tapes of her Hutcheson documentary, and they all wanted her to work for them.

She smiled, prying up a tiny flake of dead bark and dropping it into the pond. It was all very heady and confusing, especially when she was having serious doubts about staying in the television business at all. Time and again, she thought of the derision on Marsh Wheeler's face when he had taunted her about not being tough enough for the job. Maybe he was right, she brooded. Maybe she wasn't man enough for the job. She obviously didn't have the killer instinct that Marsh did, or she would have recognized Joel's exposé for the story it was and done it herself. There were other things she could do, other jobs that would give her the same satisfaction, the same sense of accomplishment. But what?

An hour later, she was no closer to an answer. She sat up wearily and held her face up to a cooling, pine-sweet breeze. *This is ridiculous,* she told herself with a trace of impatience. *Vacation's over, lady! You can't hide out from reality forever!*

Ruffian, her bay mare, gave a soft whicker. Cassidy glanced around. The horse was staring into the pines, ears pricked forward. There was an answering whicker, the soft thud of shod hoof on exposed pine root. Cassidy smiled and stretched, wondering if it was Steve or her father who had come looking for her.

But the man riding through the tall pines toward her was neither Steve nor her father. Cassidy stared with astonishment as her father's favorite long-legged chestnut gelding materialized through the sun dappled trees. Looking for all the world like one of the tall, hard-eyed heroes out of one of his own novels, Joel Logan rode toward her.

Too surprised to even move, Cassidy stared at him uncomprehendingly. He swung down off the big gelding and came to her, his handsome face set and determined. His eyes narrowed slightly as he stopped directly in front of her, legs firmly planted. He stared at her almost belligerently for a breath-held moment, and then, with no warning at all, he clasped her head in both hands, turned her face toward him and brought his mouth down over hers in a fierce, probing kiss that crushed the breath from her.

He released her finally, leaving her so stunned and dizzy that she sagged against the log for support. "My God!" she whispered. "What—what are you doing here?"

"I couldn't let it end like that, Cassidy. You're the most important thing in my life, and I'm not leaving here until I find out if you can still feel anything for me after what I've done to you."

"What you've done to me?" she echoed faintly. "But—but I was the one who—"

"You didn't do a damned thing that any other trusting, loving woman wouldn't have done. I realized that after it was too late." He smiled, his face gentling. "That was one hell of a show you did, lady."

"You saw it? I was afraid to even hope—"

"I saw it. I tried to call you when it was over, but I didn't get an answer. Then I tried calling your apartment—"

"I had the receiver off the hook."

"I called for two solid days, then finally went over and nearly pounded the damned door in. Your neighbor threatened to call the police, and when I calmed her down she told me you'd packed up Sam and had gone off somewhere. I figured you'd come here, so I tracked down the number and phoned. Some kid answered and told me you weren't here. When I told him I knew you were and wanted to talk to you, he suggested I do something impolite, and hung up."

Cassidy winced. "My brother Steve."

"Your dad answered the next time. He more or less suggested the same thing, albeit more politely, and told me not to call again. I decided the chances of wearing them down with my natural charm were damned near nil, and that if I wanted to talk to you, I was going to have to come out here to do it." He gave a snort of laughter, shaking his head. "When your menfolk get the wagons in a circle, they mean business, don't they?"

"They can be a little protective," she murmured, finally starting to realize that she wasn't simply dreaming all this. "But how...?" She gestured toward the gelding.

Joel grinned. "I had the foresight to bring along a couple of Hackamore Hayes and Dexter Kincaid first editions. Your dad decided I couldn't be all bad, saddled up the gelding and told me you were probably here."

Cassidy gave a delighted laugh. "You've made a friend for life!"

"One, anyway," he reflected with a wry smile, rubbing his jaw. "That brother of yours packs a mean right hook!"

"You don't mean—?" Cassidy's eyes widened in horror and she stepped toward him, reaching up to touch the bruise that was already starting to discolor his chin.

"He obviously doesn't share your father's enthusiasm for Hackamore Hayes," Joel muttered. "He followed me into the barn and told me he didn't like having his kid sister upset—said you were doing a lot of crying and figured I had something to do with that. He gave me a poke in the jaw for whatever I'd done in the past, and promised more of the same if I did anything to upset you today."

"Oh, Joel, I'm sorry!"

"It's all right," he told her softly. "After all, I acted like a prize jerk, thinking you'd sold me out."

"I did," she admitted in a whisper. "Oh, Joel, I'm so sorry! I was just so anxious to do the Hutcheson show that I never stopped to wonder why Marsh was so interested in you. When I heard his show that night, I felt sick. I knew what you must be thinking."

"I should have realized what had happened," he told her quietly. "I knew Marsh Wheeler and his reputation for doing anything necessary to get a story. And I knew you—or should have." He smiled wearily. "If I knew anything at all about women, I'd have known that you weren't capable of double-crossing me like that."

Cassidy stepped into his embrace, hardly believing it was true. His arms crushed her against him and she tucked her head under his chin, drinking in the reality of him. "I love you so much," she whispered. "That was the worst part, knowing I'd hurt someone I loved. Can you ever forgive me?"

There was a deep chuckle from somewhere above her. "There was never anything to forgive, you little idiot. You made a mistake; I doubled it. If anyone needs forgiving, it's me for saying the things I said, accusing you of—" He stopped, sighing. "I love you, Cass. That's really all I came up here to say. Just that I love you."

"I never even dared dream I'd ever hear you say that again," she whispered against his chest, fighting sudden tears. "Oh, Joel, I came so close to losing you. I'm giving up television for good. I'm just no good at—"

"What?" The word held a tremor of disbelieving laughter. He thrust her away from him so he could stare down at her. "What the hell are you talking about? You're one of the best, Cassidy Yorke. You don't just quit something because you made a little mistake."

"It wasn't a *little* mistake," she protested. "I ruined your life, Joel! I—"

"Oh, good God!" Joel groaned, shaking his head. "You're good, sweetheart, but don't get carried away, all right? Or more to the point, don't believe Wheeler's opinion of his own importance. His story created a bit of a sensation, but it was hardly national news."

She blinked up at him.

He grinned. "I owe Marsh Wheeler a big 'thank-you.' Ever since his story hit the air, I've become a bigger celebrity than Logan Wilde ever was. My publisher's reprinting all my novels and is planning to reactivate the Hackamore Hayes series. *People* magazine wants an interview. Two big-name publishers are trying to outbid each other on rights to my autobiography. And some studio in Hollywood's trying to convince me it would make a great movie—with me in the starring role."

"You're going to be a movie star?" she asked in astonishment.

"Not a chance!" he assured her with a smile. "I'm going back to what I love best—my writing. I won't make as much money, but with these other things there'll be enough to keep Jackie at the Hutcheson and a bit left over if I'm not extravagant. But more importantly, I'll be able to look in a mirror without wincing!" He smiled down at her. "You gave me the shove I needed, Cass. Without you I'd never have taken that first step."

Cassidy smiled dryly. "There must have been a less painful way. Although," she mused, "in a way, now it's over, I'm almost glad it happened. It made me really look at myself, too, Joel. And I don't know if I've got what it takes. I messed up in about every way possible, from falling into bed with one of my interviews to not realizing what was going on at KALB, and—"

"So you consider falling in love with me as messing up?"

"As far as my assignment goes, yes," she answered, kissing the cleft in his chin.

"You fell into bed with Joel Logan, not with Logan Wilde, remember. You weren't interviewing Joel Logan. Hell, you didn't even know Joel Logan existed."

"But—"

"You did something that mattered, Cass," he told her seriously. "You started changes that are going to be felt for years—in Albuquerque, at KALB, in yourself. Don't back off now. Don't leave the job half-done. You've got the opportunity to do something that really counts, if you've got the guts to take the challenge and run with it. Sure you messed up. You wouldn't be any good if you didn't mess up now and again. The only people who *don't* mess up are those who never try anything. Besides," he added with a grin, "if you don't come back to Albuquerque, I'm going to have to move up here to Oregon. I'm liberated enough not to mind my wife having a career, but I'll be damned if I'll put up with her having it in another state!"

"Are you asking me to marry you?" Cassidy asked in dazed astonishment.

"Sounds like it, doesn't it?"

"And Logan Wilde?" she asked, laughing. "How's a professional bachelor of his status going to explain this?"

"Logan Wilde's retired," he murmured, drawing her against him. "Permanently. From now on, the only man in your life is Joel Logan—writer, husband, loyal fan, lover. With special emphasis," he whispered with a deliciously wicked grin, "on that last one..."

"Hey, Cass?" Joel wiped his forehead with the back of his arm, looking around at her. "Where do you want this box of books?"

"Hmm?"

"Books, honey! Hundreds of the damned things!"

"What?" Cassidy looked up from the manuscript she was reading. Joel was reaching for a cardboard carton. "Oh, Joel, watch that box! The bottom's not—" At that instant Joel grasped the box and lifted it, and at the same instant the bottom gave way, spilling books and magazines over his feet. "—Solidly taped," Cassidy completed needlessly.

"Oh, hell, I give up!" Joel tossed the remains of the carton into the air and turned his back on the whole mess. "What do you say to taking a break? We've been at it for hours. Let's make a bowl of popcorn, warm up the VCR and watch a movie." He grinned. "Maybe neck a little."

"Yeah, okay," Cassidy murmured absently. "Do you want to stop this for a while?"

"Cassie, Cassie—what am I going to do with you?"

"What?" She looked up.

"I said," Joel repeated firmly, walking toward her, "that it's time we took a break."

"Good idea." Cassidy closed the manuscript on her finger and smiled up at her husband. He was wearing a pair of blue jeans that had seen better days, and a faded plaid work shirt, and he looked damp and tousled. "You look tired."

"Not surprisingly, considering we've spent the day clearing out your apartment and mine and bringing everything out here."

"True." She looked around her with a sigh. She was sitting cross-legged in the middle of the living room floor of the cabin, surrounded by packing boxes and odd pieces of furniture they hadn't found room for yet. Buster was stretched out asleep on the hearth, while Sam and Joel's black cat eyed each other mistrustfully from either end of the long sofa. "We can sleep in tomorrow morning. There's supposed to be a bad snowstorm tonight."

"Good." Joel grinned wickedly. "With any kind of luck, we'll be snowed in for a week. We can stay in bed and call it a honeymoon."

"We *had* a honeymoon. Hawaii, remember?"

"Yeah, but that was nearly three months ago." He sprawled beside her, reaching out to give Sam a pat. Startled, the cat growled and shot off the sofa to sulk under the nearest table, rumbling threateningly.

"Oh, shut up, Sam," Cassidy told her calmly. "You may as well get used to communal living, because this is your home from now on."

"You seem to have adapted pretty well." Joel wiped a smudge of dust from her cheek.

"Yes, I have, haven't I?" Cassidy looked around her contentedly. "Considering that I came into this time-honored institution with nominal skills in any of the wifely arts."

"Oh, there's at least one wifely art in which you've proved proficient," Joel reminded her with a slow smile. "In fact, you've excelled at it."

"Cooking?" Cassidy asked innocently. "I haven't burned anything too badly in over a week now."

"That wasn't really what I was thinking about," Joel murmured, kissing her ear. He turned his head, trying to see what she was reading. "What is that, anyway? You've had your nose in that magazine for over an hour."

"It's a manuscript." She turned it so he could see the title page. "One of yours."

"*Wilde Women: How To Make Love To Your Man*. Where did you find that?"

"In one of the boxes of stuff we brought up from your apartment." She flipped it open to the page she had been reading, sliding Joel a mischievous glance through her lashes. "It's very interesting. Too bad you didn't finish it."

"Why are you looking at me like that?"

"Oh, I was just thinking that it would be a shame to have this here and not put it to some good use."

"It would make good kindling."

Cassidy set the manuscript aside, rocking up onto her knees. She started unbuttoning Joel's work shirt. "That's not the kind of fire I was thinking about starting, Mr. Logan. You said you wanted to take a break from unpacking."

"So I did," he murmured encouragingly. "What chapter were you reading?"

Smiling, Cassidy pulled the shirt out of his jeans and finished unbuttoning it. She slipped it over his shoulders and arms and tossed it aside, then put her hands on his shoulders and gently but firmly pushed him over backward. "I was planning on starting on page one, chapter one," she whispered, starting to kiss his throat and chest, "and working my way through to the end. It could take us weeks." She touched his flat nipple with her tongue, then put her mouth over it fully. She circled it repeatedly with her tongue and Joel's breathing became slightly unsteady. She ran her palm down his hard, flat stomach. The metal button on his jeans slid free and Cassidy inched the zipper down one tooth at a time, stringing a wandering row of biting little kisses from his chest to his navel. She paused there to dip her tongue delicately into its depths and Joel's breath hissed.

"Cass..."

"Lie still," she whispered. "Just lie still and let me love you." She worked the jeans down over his hips and legs, following their downward journey with more kisses. Nuzzling his bare foot, she drew circles on his sole with her tongue until Joel laughingly begged her to stop, then started working her way back up. She slid off his briefs in the same manner, and by the time he lay naked on the thick braided rug her own body was afire in anticipation. Slowly, she started kissing his lower stomach, biting the tender skin gently. Her hair spilled over him and he flinched, groaning softly when she moved her kisses lower still.

Joel arched his back slightly, hands clenched at his sides, as that playful kiss became an intimate caress. "What are you doing to me?"

"You should know," she murmured with a chuckle. "You wrote the book, remember."

"Oh, sweetheart!"

Laughing quietly, she sat back on her heels. Joel was watching her, eyes sultry under the half-lowered lids, and she held that burning gaze as she slowly started removing her own dusty shirt and jeans.

"I love you, Mrs. Logan."

"And I love you, Mr. Logan," Cassidy whispered, slipping astride him. "Very, very much . . ."

"Cass—Cass!" Joel reached for her. "Darling, do you think we should be doing this?"

"You mean this?" Cassidy asked with a throaty laugh, easing herself down over him so gently that Joel groaned in pleasure. "Or this? Or what about this?" She moved slowly on him, hands on his waist.

"Cass, sweetheart—" Teeth gritted, he reached down and placed his hand on her stomach. "Is it safe?"

Cassidy looked down at her flat, trim belly, and started to laugh. "Good grief, he's barely eight weeks old, Joel! Surely you're not planning on abstaining from your husbandly duties for the next seven months!"

He grinned. "I was hoping not to, but this is all pretty new to me."

"It's pretty new to me, too," she reminded him with a laugh. "Jack Crothers is pretty upset with you, by the way. He's still old-fashioned enough to believe that a woman can't work and raise babies, too. I told him I'd work full-time until Josh is born, then part-time until he starts school." She smiled. "He wants to know how we managed this."

"I have a feeling," Joel said, groaning, "that it started something like this."

"You know," Cassidy whispered, closing her eyes with an intake of breath as Joel started moving under her, "I think your good friend Logan Wilde might have been on to something."